The WOMEN of CYPRESS LANE

A NOVEL

JANINE LANGE

LITTLE BLACK BOOK
PUBLISHING

St. Louis, MO

Published by LBB Publishing. An imprint of Little Black Book: Women in Business

Editing by Karen L. Tucker, Comma Queen Editing

Cover, interior, and layout design by Shelly Snow Pordea

Paperback ISBN 978-1-962417-38-9

Ebook ISBN 978-1-962417-37-2

Library of Congress Control Number: 2026909817

CONTENTS

To my family—those who came before me and those who are present in my life now. You have taught me that *Home* is much more than just a place to hold possessions; it's where love, encouragement, and inspiration flourish. Wherever life takes me, I carry my *Home* within my heart, a constant light guiding my way.

Chapter One

THE 750-MILE DRIVE FROM New York to South Carolina was grueling. The burning tears in Laney's eyes blurred the white lines in the road, making it difficult to navigate the lonely highway. She wanted to get home as quickly as possible, as thoughts of the life-changing phone call consumed her with agonizing pain and grief. *How could this have happened? It couldn't be true. Is she really gone?*

New York, New York – 1989

Laney arrived at her apartment building a little past midnight after a busier-than-usual night at the restaurant. She wanted nothing more than a hot shower and to drop into bed. Hearing the phone ringing from the hallway outside her apartment, Laney fumbled with her keys to unlock the door. She rushed inside to pick up the phone, noticing the blinking lights on her answering machine signifying several messages. "Hello, this is Laney," she said, catching her breath and hoping she'd made it in time.

"Miss Armstrong?" the unfamiliar voice on the other end asked.

"Yes, this is Laney Armstrong," she told the caller.

"My name is Julie Fisher, and I'm a nurse at Roper Hospital in Charleston," she explained. Laney's heart sank as she sat down on the sofa, sensing that this couldn't be good news at this late hour. "Miss Armstrong," the nurse continued, "Ivy Westfield is your grandmother, is that correct?"

"Yes," Laney replied. "Is she okay? Has something happened to her?"

"I'm so sorry to tell you that Mrs. Westfield passed away this evening," said the nurse.

Shocked and confused, Laney asked her to repeat what she had said.

"The ambulance brought Mrs. Westfield into the emergency room with chest pains. The doctors attended to her for over an hour but couldn't save her. She died from congestive heart failure at 6:45 p.m. Since you were listed as her next of kin, we've been trying to reach you for the last few hours. Please accept my deepest condolences, Miss Armstrong."

A myriad of thoughts entered her mind. *There must be some mistake.* It was only three months ago that Ivy came to New York to spend Christmas with Laney. Ivy's energy and stamina to keep up with the hectic pace were impressive. They attended the spectacular show at Radio City Music Hall, watched the skaters at Rockefeller Center, and walked to St. Patrick's Cathedral. They dined at their favorite restaurant and later enjoyed the dazzling holiday displays in Macy's windows. Ivy never let on that she had a heart condition.

After receiving the call from the hospital, Laney called Ivy's neighbor and good friend, Marjorie Buchanan, to see if she had heard the news.

"Yes, Laney, I know about your grandmother, and I'm so sorry, dear. In fact, I was with her today."

Laney listened as Marjorie told her the details about what had happened.

"It had been a pleasant afternoon, and Ivy was outside cleaning up overgrown weeds around the hydrangea bushes near the front porch. She never got around to the fall cleanup last year, and insisted on pulling the weeds and pruning the bushes to prepare for the spring season. Mr. Buchanan offered to help her, but she told him she wanted to do it herself."

"That sounds like my grandmother."

"In the early evening, our dog came running toward the house barking excessively. I followed him back to Ivy's house and found her lying on the sidewalk, unconscious. I called the ambulance at once and they took her to the hospital, where she died a little while later."

Laney started crying at the thought of her grandmother all alone at the hospital when she died.

"I tried to call you, Laney, but got your answering machine."

"I'm so sorry I missed your call. I worked late tonight."

"It's not your fault, Laney. How could you have known something like this would happen?"

Early the next day, Laney set plans in motion to leave for South Carolina. Her boss readily agreed to a two-week leave of absence from her job. She arranged for her friends to pick up her mail and watch over her apartment. Determined to make it to Charleston that evening, Laney drove for twelve straight hours, stopping only for fast food, coffee, and using the restroom.

Charleston, SC – 1989

Laney pulled off the highway at eleven that night, relieved to be near her childhood home. With less than a mile to go, the car began to sputter and choke before coming to an abrupt stop. She tried to start it again, but it wouldn't turn over.

What's wrong now? The dashboard lights are still lit, so it can't be a dead battery.

She glanced at the red arrow on the gas gauge pointing below the "E" line. *Oh no! How could I have forgotten to fill up the car when I passed the last gas station?*

Furious at herself for being so absent-minded, Laney had no choice but to get out and walk the rest of the way to Ivy's house. Darkness cloaked the remote country road as Laney began her trek with only a small flashlight to guide her way. She walked a short distance when she heard a pickup truck approaching, stopping just before reaching her. She shielded her eyes from the headlights and moved to the side of the road. A tall, stocky man dressed in denim jeans and boots exited the truck and walked her way.

"Hello," the man called out. "Car trouble?"

"More like driver trouble," Laney quipped nervously. "I forgot these things need to be refilled with gas to keep going."

The man came closer, but the blinding headlights shining behind him obliterated Laney's view of his face. He kept his truck running, making it difficult to hear his voice. With a hint of laughter, the tall man said, "Cars are funny that way, aren't they?"

An uneasy feeling about being alone and stranded on a dark road set in. Sensing her trepidation, the man kept an appropriate distance.

"I can help you. I live down the road aways," he offered.

"Thank you so much. I'm on my way to my grandmother's house, but hadn't quite made it," said Laney.

The man asked, "Laney, is that you?"

"Chase? Yes, it's me."

"I can't believe it. When I saw the car on the side of the road, I had no idea it would be you!"

Relief washed over Laney when she realized the man standing before her was Chase Buchanan, her oldest and dearest friend. Overcome with exhaustion, Laney collapsed into Chase's arms. He embraced her for a minute or two before letting go.

Laney and Chase went back a long way, having been neighbors and friends since they were small children. Laney was only four years old when her grandmother, Ivy Westfield, took her in to live with her and raise her on her own. Tragically, Laney's parents were killed in a fiery car crash. Ivy, being Laney's closest living relative, became her legal guardian. She showered Laney with love and affection but also managed to be a disciplinarian and parental figure all rolled into one. She taught Laney the importance of family, commitment, and responsibility, but most of all, unconditional love. Despite having lost both her parents at such an early age, Laney had been a relatively happy, well-adjusted child.

Laney had learned a great deal from her grandmother about other things as well, such as managing a household and tending to a garden large enough to sustain them with plenty of fruits, vegetables, and herbs. Ivy also shared her love of flowers, which could make a beautiful display inside or out. She taught Laney how to prepare the soil, start seedlings in late winter, and sow them when the spring weather signaled the start of the growing season.

Ivy did her best to run the household and gardens; however, it became a little too much for her to manage by herself with the added responsibility of raising a little girl. Her brother Preston lived nearby, but he disdained physical labor and wasn't much help. Each year, she hired a few men to help her with the growing season in return for room, board, and meals. The arrangement suited both Ivy and the men she employed. They watched out for Laney, too. One time in particular, Laney chased a kitten up into the hayloft. When she lost her footing on the ladder and fell, one of the workers caught her before she hit the floor, saving her from serious injury.

Laney often wandered to a secluded hideaway she had discovered while exploring her grandmother's estate. It sat just beyond the pond at the farthest part of the property under a tall cypress tree. Laney loved to escape to this private sanctuary where she could be alone with her thoughts and dreams.

She frequently imagined what her life would be like if she had a mother and father like all her friends from school. She conjured images of her mother sitting beside her, braiding her long blonde hair and reading her favorite story aloud. She pictured her father fishing in the pond and joining them to share a basket lunch of fried chicken and homemade biscuits washed down with cool, sweet lemonade. But, as usual, when Laney opened her eyes, the harsh reality of her life set in. She had no parents. She loved living with Grandma Ivy in this big, beautiful house, but always harbored a longing inside that no amount of love could quell.

Once, Laney's imagination got away from her, and she thought she saw her father visiting Ivy's house. She vaguely remembered him from a photo her mother used to keep on her dresser. The picture was worn and faded, so she couldn't be certain it was the same man. Uncle Preston was there, and the vehement arguing between him and the man scared Laney. She heard him tell the man to stay away, "or else."

Being too afraid to go near the house, Laney went to the Buchanans' to hide out for a while. She waited until everyone left and things quieted down before returning home. Later on, she asked Grandma Ivy about the man, and she told Laney it was an acquaintance of Uncle Preston's. The man never appeared again, and Laney brushed it off as her mind inventing stories her heart wanted to believe were true.

Another time, Laney lazily closed her eyes for a short nap in the warmth of the afternoon sun when she felt something tickling her bare foot. She kicked away what she assumed was a blade of grass or an inquisitive ladybug and turned to her side. Once again, the tingling sensation ran up the side of one foot and down the other. She opened her eyes and, to her astonishment, found a boy sitting on the grass teasing her foot with a twig. She jumped up and started to scream.

"Who are you and what are you doing here?"

"Pipe down! Do you want to scare every animal in the county?"

"I'll scream even louder if you come near me!"

Amused by her girlish reaction, the boy said, "Silly girl, I'm Chase Buchanan, your neighbor. I live right next door in the house over there." He pointed to a modest clapboard house sitting beyond the trees that bordered the two properties. "We go to the same school, but I'm two classes ahead of you."

Laney recognized the boy from school but had never had an occasion to talk to him. She didn't realize he lived so close to her grandmother's house.

"What's your name?" asked Chase, even though he already knew it. Chase's parents were friends with Ivy, and they had told him all about her granddaughter coming to live with her after her parents' accident. He had seen her a time or two but didn't have the courage to venture off his property to talk to her until today.

"I'm Laney Armstrong. I live here with my Grandma Ivy."

And so, the friendship between Chase and Laney began. Neither of them had brothers or sisters. They spent their summers exploring the woods together, swimming in the pond, catching frogs and fireflies, and enjoying whatever adventures the two of them could find. They were best buddies and developed an easygoing friendship.

Chase taught Laney how to ride a bicycle, and Laney taught Chase how to make s'mores in the firepit. Sometimes, Ivy would pack them a lunch as they headed off on one of their afternoon explorations. On Halloween, Chase's dad would treat them to a hayride through the cornfields with some of the other kids in the county. They held pumpkin-carving contests, and Chase's mom baked chocolate chip cookies and served apple cider for everyone to enjoy. At night, they sang around a campfire under the stars. Laney couldn't help but envy Chase for having both his parents and considered herself fortunate to be included as part of his family.

Chase started high school two years ahead of Laney. Good-looking and kind, all the girls vied for his attention. His involvement in sports and his role in helping his father oversee the farm and livestock left little time for dating. Being their only son, Chase's parents expected him to help work the land his great-grandfather had settled almost one hundred years ago. They had cattle, hogs, and chickens, and grew corn, grains, and soybeans. Although smaller in size compared to others in the area, the farm afforded their family a decent living, and Chase and his dad could manage it together.

When Laney entered her freshman year, she began to see Chase differently. As a teenager, new and unfamiliar emotions stirred inside her whenever their paths crossed. She became quite annoyed with herself whenever feelings of jealousy erupted seeing Chase talk with another girl. *This is just plain nonsense. Chase is my best friend, not my boyfriend!*

Chase, on the other hand, considered himself more like an older brother to Laney, always watching out for her and making sure she stayed safe. As Laney matured, she observed him becoming more handsome every day. *Has he noticed that I'm not a little girl anymore?* she wondered.

After high school, they lost touch when each went their separate ways to attend college. In Laney's junior year, Chase left Charleston to attend Clemson University, majoring in Agricultural Business Management. Two years later, Laney accepted an offer from the Culinary Institute of America in Hyde Park, New York, and moved away a few months after graduation.

Now, here they stood eight years later, meeting in the middle of the road on a dark night. Chase knew Laney was here because of Ivy's passing and offered his condolences.

"I'm so sorry about Ivy, Lane."

"Thank you, Chase." Laney stood still, frozen from the stress of the news and the long drive. Chase broke the awkward silence.

"Let's get you up to Ivy's house. I'll swing back around tomorrow and put some gas in your car."

"I don't want to put you to any trouble, Chase. I can—"

Chase cut her off mid-sentence. "Nonsense," he said, unwavering in his offer. "You know me better than that, Lane."

Laney didn't have the energy or willingness to argue with him. In fact, she was relieved she didn't have to deal with it tonight. "Thank you. I appreciate this more than you know."

"No problem. Do you have a suitcase you want me to grab for you?"

Laney popped open the trunk, and Chase got her bag out and put it in the back of his pickup. She climbed into the cab, and they drove the short distance down the road to Ivy's house.

"I hope you don't mind, but I didn't know how soon you'd be back, so I came by to secure the house. How long will you be here?"

"I took two weeks off, but will be staying longer if necessary. It's going to be strange being in the house without my grandmother."

"You're more than welcome to stay at our house. I know my mom and dad would love to have you."

"I appreciate that, but I think I'll be okay."

He wasn't convinced but didn't argue the point. They pulled into the driveway, and Chase helped Laney out of the truck. He got her suitcase and escorted her to the front door, leaving his headlights on to light the dark path.

"Why don't you at least come over for dinner after you get settled in?"

"I might just take you up on that offer. It's been a rough twenty-four hours, and I'd love to see your parents."

"Great, I'll let my mom know," said Chase, pleased that Laney accepted. "Call me if you need anything before then. My number's still the same."

"It's nice to know you're right down the road, like always," said Laney, thankful for the nearness of old, familiar friends.

She smiled, gave him a hug, and walked up the front steps into the dark, deserted house.

Laney entered the foyer and went straight upstairs to her old room, purposely keeping the door to Ivy's room closed to avoid the sight of her grandmother's empty bed. Depleted from the long drive, she lay down on her bed still wearing her clothes.

Ten hours later, the bright orange glow of the sun illuminated Laney's bedroom. It took a few minutes for Laney's mind to register waking up in South Carolina in her grandmother's house and not in her apartment in New York. Despite being alone in the empty house, a sense of consolation enveloped her.

Chapter Two

Charleston, SC – 1989

LANEY GOT DRESSED AND made her way downstairs to the kitchen. Finding only a box of stale graham crackers and peanut butter in the cupboards, she wished she had a cold glass of milk to go along with it. *This will have to do until I can get to the grocery store.*

Laney hadn't been back home in quite some time. Now, as she roamed the house with fresh eyes, it appeared to be a bit run-down inside and out, with no updates since the early 1960s. The white, sheer Priscilla curtains hanging in the dining room windows remained unchanged for as long as Laney could remember, and the green, pebbled linoleum kitchen floor was worn and faded.

Outside, the house appeared weathered and neglected. Laney imagined the house in its heyday in all its majesty. She envisioned the hydrangeas full and vibrant with their cobalt-colored petals rich with a sweet aroma. As her gaze drifted to the lattice trellis, flanked on both sides by pale purple lilac bushes, she remembered dodging bumblebees attracted to the sweet nectar of the dense spring flowers.

Memories of sitting on the expansive wraparound porch on a warm summer evening, sipping iced tea filled her mind. Closing her eyes, she pictured herself running out to the front yard with the screen door banging behind her. Her grandmother shouted not to slam the door in vain. Laney would run outside in a flash, spinning on the swing that hung from the massive oak tree overlooking the pond.

Those carefree days reminded Laney of happier times in her life. She pushed past the memories that tugged at her heartstrings to get on with the task at hand, planning her grandmother's burial.

At Ivy's request, no funeral would be held. She would be buried in the cemetery next to her beloved husband, Henry Westfield. Laney honored Ivy's wishes and made the arrangements. She planned to hold a small gathering at a later date to celebrate Ivy's life with her friends and neighbors.

After leaving the funeral home, Laney stopped to pick up some groceries. She called her answering machine back in her apartment and listened to a message from Mr. James Gallagher, urging her to call him regarding her grandmother's estate.

The receptionist at Gallagher & Gallagher recognized Laney's name and put the call through to James.

"Thank you for calling me back, Miss Armstrong. I'm the attorney handling Mrs. Westfield's estate and would like to set up a time to meet with you regarding her last will and testament."

In all the commotion of the last two days, Laney never gave a thought to a will. Caught off guard, she replied, "Yes, of course, Mr. Gallagher. I'm staying at my grandmother's house and will be here for at least another week or so. What day is convenient for you?"

They arranged to meet the following Monday, giving Laney the weekend to rest.

James Gallagher rang the doorbell at 2 p.m. on the dot. He looked lawyerly. Tall and well-dressed in a Brooks Brothers suit and tie, polished Oxford shoes, and coiffed hair, Laney guessed his age to be in the late forties or early fifties.

"Miss Armstrong, I presume," he said as he shook her hand with a firm grip. "I'm James Gallagher. We spoke on the phone. It's a pleasure to meet you."

"Same here," Laney replied, wincing as his overzealous handshake pinched her fingers. "Please come in."

Laney held the screen door open, allowing Mr. Gallagher to pass in front of her. The overpowering scent of his cologne knocked her back a step. She led him into the dining room, and they both took a seat at the table. Mr. Gallagher removed a tidy stack of paperwork from his briefcase and spread it out on the table in front of them so they could review the documents together.

"Now, Miss Armstrong," he started.

"Please, call me Laney."

"Very well then, Laney, I'm here as the legal representative for your grandmother Ivy Westfield's estate."

Just the words "Ivy Westfield's estate" sent a chill down Laney's spine. She struggled with the realization that her grandmother wouldn't be cooking in the kitchen anymore, napping on the front porch swing, or working in the vegetable garden. Laney wouldn't hear Ivy's voice singing along with Frank Sinatra on the radio or watch her hips swaying to the music as she reminisced about dancing with her husband Hank so many years ago.

James's abrupt "ahem" snapped Laney back to the reality of the distasteful business of settling her legal affairs.

"I apologize, Mr. Gallagher. It's tough being in this house since my grandmother passed away. It's hard not to get lost in the memories."

"No need to apologize, I understand. Would you rather reschedule for another time?"

"No. You've come this far, and I wouldn't want you to make the trip again because of me."

Being all business, James Gallagher acknowledged Laney's desire to continue and proceeded to read the Last Will and Testament of Ivy Westfield. It appeared to be a rather short document, much to Laney's relief. The quicker they could get through this, the better.

"I, Ivy Westfield, being of sound mind and body, do hereby bequeath all my worldly possessions listed below to my granddaughter, Laney Armstrong." The list included the house and all its contents, all the property, her car, jewelry, savings and checking accounts, and so on. The total monetary inheritance amounted to just shy of $950,000.

James Gallagher continued reading, but once again, Laney became lost in her thoughts. It hadn't occurred to Laney until that moment that this house now belonged to her. She never expected to own a home at this point in her life, let alone receive a sizable inheritance. Laney wasn't surprised, though; her grandmother was thrifty and a fanatic about reusing and recycling whatever she could long before it became popular to do so. It all seemed too much to comprehend.

Fading back to the sound of James Gallagher's voice, she picked up his last line where he said Ivy had left a letter for Laney. He explained that Ivy had written the letter and included it in the will to be given to Laney at the appropriate time. He handed her a plain white envelope with writing on the front.

In her grandmother's familiar handwriting, she read the words, "To my Laney girl," Ivy's pet name for her. Her eyes immediately filled with tears. Laney kept a box of birthday and holiday cards as well as sentimental notes from Ivy, but she sensed the importance and serious nature of this letter. Being a gentleman, James excused himself and went out to the porch to give Laney a chance to regain her composure. Laney sat with the letter in her hand and decided to wait until later to read it. She would need a strong cup of tea and a box of tissues for this one.

Mr. Gallagher returned, and Laney asked, "Is there anything else I need to do?"

"Not at this time. The transfer of possessions will be completed in about two weeks, but legally, you own everything now, so you can do as you please with it. Here's my card. I'm sure you will have questions once the dust settles and you've had time to digest all that has happened."

"Thank you, Mr. Gallagher. I appreciate your help."

"Your grandmother was my client for many years, and I'm more than willing to be of service to her only living descendant."

Mr. Gallagher gathered up his briefcase and headed for his car, reiterating that she could contact him at any time. She thanked him again, and he drove away, leaving Laney alone in the house.

Laney tried to reconcile what had happened in the last few days, all of it so sudden and unexpected. She thought Ivy would live to be at least one hundred and not die at the age of sixty-seven. Always stoic and strong, Ivy never admitted to being in pain or to any other problem that might have slowed her down. Now that she was gone and had left everything to Laney; there were many life-changing decisions to make.

Living and working in New York, Laney was satisfied with her life; however, at times, she felt lonely and isolated without friends or family nearby.

Another surprising event was seeing Chase again. It felt as if they had just seen each other last week, not over eight years ago. She had kept up on his life through Ivy and heard that he lived on the same property as his parents. He built a small house for himself on the far end of their eighty acres. Ivy had never mentioned a girlfriend, and Laney wondered if Chase was involved with anyone. She looked forward to dinner with Chase and his parents and hoped to fill in some of the blanks.

Later that afternoon, Laney made herself a strong cup of tea and went upstairs to the sitting room next to Ivy's bedroom. She took out the letter and stared at the words on the envelope:

To my Laney girl.

Drawing a deep breath, Laney began reading the letter penned in her grandmother's distinctive handwriting:

As you read this letter, my dear Laney, I hope you can do so without too much sadness or grief. I always tried to teach you

that grieving is a natural part of life, something we all endure at some point. My hope is that you find comfort in knowing that you forever hold a special place in my heart. I loved you from the first minute I laid eyes on you and treasured raising you. Watching you grow and blossom to become the woman you are today reminded me of a younger version of myself. Your resilience and zest for living are part of what kept me going all these years.

I've seen to it that you have plenty of money to pursue your dreams and live a full and happy life. The house is now yours too. It has seen good times and bad, joy and sorrow, hardship and prosperity. A place to celebrate life, honor tradition, and nurture those who live under its roof. It's your legacy, Laney girl, and part of what makes you who you are today. It would be wonderful if you returned to live in your childhood home and perhaps raise a family of your own here, just as Henry and I started out to do so many years ago.

There is something I need to tell you, Laney, and I pray you will understand. When you were about eight years old, a man came to the house, and you asked me who he was. I kept the truth about the man's true identity from you. He was your father.

We were all led to believe that Peter Armstrong died in the car crash that took your mother from us, but somehow, he survived and went into hiding. I was shocked when he showed up one day and attempted to extort money from me. He threatened to take you away from me, which I could never have allowed.

Peter was a mean drunk who never treated you or your mother right. I had to protect you from that horrible man and save you from a life of misery like your mother had endured. I was faced with the choice of letting you know he was alive and risking him hurting you, or finding a way to be rid of him for good. I asked Preston to take care of it, and he told me I wouldn't have to worry about it anymore. I never saw or heard from Peter again. Preston wouldn't say what had happened, and I didn't ask. Still, I've always wondered what actually happened and if my actions had dire consequences.

Keeping you from knowing your father was one of the most difficult decisions I had to make. Your well-being and safety were my only priorities, and I acted in your best interest. This secret has haunted me for years. I want you to know that I'm truly sorry. Hopefully, on my day of atonement, God will forgive me as I hope you will too.

I pray you will be happy and live your life to the fullest. Remember the special moments we shared together, keep them close in your heart, and know I will always be a part of you.

Your loving Grandmother

Laney's hands trembled as she held the letter, rereading it several times. *I did see my father that day! It wasn't a dream or a fantasy.* At first, she wanted to scream at Ivy for keeping the truth from her. But forcing herself to travel back in time to a painful place, Laney understood her grandmother's motives and the decision she had made.

She recalled the fighting, the screaming, and the terrifying sound of glass breaking as dishes were thrown against the wall by her father while her mother wrapped her protective arms around Laney to shelter her from harm. She remembered her and her mother locking themselves in the back bedroom to wait until her father stormed out of the house, signaling they'd be safe to come out. After all these years, these horrific images remained indelibly etched in her mind.

Chapter Three

Charleston, SC – 1989

NOTHING COULD DIMINISH LANEY'S love for Ivy, not even this long-held secret about her father's existence. Laney had a wonderful childhood thanks to her grandmother—much different from living in constant fear of her father's temper. Ivy had doted on Laney; she held her during times of loneliness, sewed dresses for her dolls, and hosted elaborate tea parties for her stuffed animals. Together, they went to the ocean for vacations and made castles in the sand. Ivy ensured Laney had all she needed but never spoiled her.

When Laney started school, Ivy volunteered for the PTA, donated money to the new gymnasium fund, and hosted the annual school picnics at her home. Her property easily accommodated enough tables to seat the entire class, their parents, and all the teachers. Ivy arranged pony rides and a magician to perform for the children. Many of Ivy's classmates commented that they wished they had a grandmother like Laney's, which always made her feel good.

After graduating high school, Laney faced the difficult decision of whether to attend a college close to Charleston or the Culinary Institute of America in Hyde Park, New York, one of the best schools in the country. Knowing her love of cooking, Ivy urged Laney to pursue her dream of becoming a chef.

"But, Grandma, it's so far away, and I don't know anyone in New York."

"It's only for four years, and it's close enough to drive home for long weekends, spring breaks, or summer vacations. You have your whole life ahead of you, Laney girl, and this is a wonderful opportunity to learn your craft and achieve your goals."

"Do you think it's best for me, Grandma?"

"I do."

Sitting alone on the bank of the pond, Laney contemplated going away to school. From a young age, Laney was inspired by her grandmother's skill for creating delicious meals and hosting wonderful dinner parties. She had watched Ivy's every move in the kitchen, learning her techniques and picking up tips and tricks. Now, as an adult, she wanted to hone her skills. Having lived in Charleston her entire life, the idea of moving to New York sparked a thrilling sense of adventure within her. She'd have her own apartment and could pursue the career of her dreams. After much thought, Laney decided she would go to New York.

On the day of Laney's high school graduation, Ivy surprised her with a brand-new car, a shiny red Mustang. Laney couldn't contain herself when she opened the front door and saw it sitting in the driveway with a big white bow on its hood.

"Grandma, is that for me?" She ran to the driveway, opened the car door, and jumped inside.

"Yes, my dear, it's all yours. I'm so proud of you for graduating with honors. You need a reliable car for all those trips back and forth from New York to home."

"Get in, Grandma, let's go for a ride!"

They took off down the road in Laney's new car. Ivy hoped this first voyage would be the start of many adventures Laney would take in her lifetime, and she relished sharing this moment with her.

Soon, the time came for Laney to leave for school. Ivy paid her tuition and secured an apartment close to campus. One of Ivy's friends in New York found the apartment and reassured her that the neighborhood was safe for a young girl living on her own. She promised to check in on Laney from time to time. Knowing her granddaughter would have someone to turn to in case of an emergency brought Ivy a sense of relief.

Ivy packed a lunch and some soft drinks for Laney to take on the long trip. She made her promise to stop every couple of hours to take breaks and stretch her legs. Laney planned to drive about halfway to Richmond, Virginia, and spend the night there. The next day, she would complete the trip and arrive in New York after lunchtime. Ivy asked Laney to check in along the way and call her when she reached Virginia.

Laney put her suitcase and a few small boxes of personal belongings in the trunk. She turned to her grandmother and hugged her.

"I love you, Laney girl. Now go and start your new adventure. Don't worry about me. I'll be fine here, like I've always been. Besides, the Buchanans are a stone's throw from my front door."

"I love you too, Grandma. I'll be looking forward to your coming to New York in three weeks for Parents' Weekend."

Laney became entrenched in her new life and flourished. She excelled in school and made friends with a handful of girls. Together, they enjoyed exploring the sights and sounds of the city.

As promised, Laney traveled home often, her independence and confidence growing with each visit. After graduation, Laney accepted a fantastic job in a restaurant on the Upper East Side of Manhattan as an apprentice chef. Her skills earned her a promotion to sous chef in a mere six months. She created new dishes and developed menu options, eliciting rave reviews from diners and critics. She enjoyed her job and made a name for herself in the culinary circles of New York City.

Being home in the familiar surroundings of Charleston evoked feelings of nostalgia and a connection to her past. Laney hadn't contemplated making any changes in her life until now that she owned the house she grew up in. Ivy's presence could be seen everywhere in the little knick-knacks, paintings, and personal touches scattered about. Ivy liked collecting figurines of birds and proudly displayed them. She loved inexpensive items purchased from the local five-and-dime store as much as her mother's fine china. Ivy also loved table linens and had a different one for each occasion. Lace scarves and doilies dotted her dresser and night tables. Laney loved the old-fashioned décor and cherished all of Ivy's belongings.

Should I make such a drastic move and return to my childhood home? Given the house's dilapidated condition, the thought overwhelmed her. The exterior needed mostly cosmetic work to restore it to its original grand appearance. The inside, however, would require a complete renovation from plumbing to electric to heating and air conditioning. She started making a mental list of what needed to be done.

The sound of a truck pulling into the driveway broke her concentration. She walked out on the front porch to find Chase's truck parked alongside her Mustang.

"Sure is a mighty pretty pony you have here, Laney. I have to admit, I was tempted to take her for a spin when I brought it back."

"She is powerful. I would be lying if I said I never raced down the highway at almost a hundred miles an hour for the thrill of it!"

Laney's confession surprised Chase, and he returned the smile. They both turned their gaze toward the house.

"I imagine the house belongs to you, Laney, now that Ivy is..."

"Yes, it does."

"What do you think you'll do?"

"I'm not sure, Chase. It's been a whirlwind of revelations and emotions that I need to sort through."

"I understand, Laney. I wasn't trying to push you. My mom would like you to come over about five o'clock tonight for dinner. She's baking her famous apple pie that you love so much."

"I'll be there with bells on."

Laney looked forward to dinner at the Buchanans', not only to visit with them, but to take her mind off Ivy's letter. She decided she wouldn't mention its contents or any implications it may hold.

Laney arrived at the Buchanans' at five o'clock sharp. She had picked up a bouquet of flowers and a bottle of wine for her hosts. Mrs. Buchanan hugged Laney as she came through the front door, and Chase's dad followed suit. A rambunctious

Golden Retriever joined the welcoming committee, offering Laney a slobbery kiss on her face when she bent down to pet him.

"Meet Buddy," Chase said as he tried to corral the dog.

"Great to see you, Laney," Mrs. Buchanan exclaimed. "I'm so sorry about your grandmother. We all loved Ivy."

Chase's dad added, "Your grandmother was such a fine lady. Folks like that are hard to come by these days."

"Thank you, Mr. Buchanan. You're right about that."

Moving into the dining room, Buddy took his place under the table close to Chase. A delicious, home-cooked meal was exactly what Laney needed. The apple pie reminded her of many dinners she had enjoyed at the Buchanans' home as a kid. They spent the evening talking about the past eight years and the goings-on in each other's lives. The Buchanans asked Laney about her life in New York and her career as a chef.

"It's very exciting. I love making a mouth-watering dish out of ingredients most people would not expect to find on the same plate."

"You can cook for me anytime you want, Laney!" said Chase's father.

"I can't hold a candle to your wife's down-home cooking, Mr. B."

She turned her attention to Chase. "You haven't had much to say. What's life been like for you since I left Charleston?"

Nonchalantly, Chase told her that he had earned a degree and returned to work for his father.

Mr. Buchanan added, "He left out a few parts, including how he built his own house, saved the farm from going under after we had lost most of our crops to the drought last year, and turned down a high-paying job offer from the Farm Bureau of South Carolina."

Chase looked uncomfortable and glossed over his dad's accolades. "If you listen to him, I should be running for president."

Laney smiled warmly at Chase, appreciating his modesty as his father expressed his pride in him. Throughout the conversation, she noted that no one mentioned a girlfriend, so she assumed that Chase was single.

After dinner, Buddy's scratching at the back door signaled he was ready for a walk or, more aptly, a run. Mrs. Buchanan told Chase and Laney that she would clean up the dishes so they could enjoy the last hour or so of daylight. Laney offered to help, but Chase's mom wouldn't hear of it.

"Shoo, shoo, you two," she said as she pushed them out the door.

The pleasant evening boasted a pale purple sky, catching the tail end of daylight before dusk. Chase attempted to keep Buddy on a leash but gave up after his constant tugging and pulling.

"That dog will be the death of me!"

"I like him, Chase. I've always wanted a dog of my own, but New York City isn't a great place to raise a pet."

They walked a little farther and ended up by the pond on Ivy's property. They sat side by side on the dock with their legs dangling over the edge.

"Do you remember our picnics and scavenger hunts around here, Laney?"

"Of course, I do! Those are some of my favorite memories. We go back a long way, don't we, Chase?"

"Yeah, I always liked that about you and me. We've been friends forever, it seems."

Chase sat less than an inch from Laney. She liked the woodsy scent of his aftershave—not overpowering like the lawyer's cologne. She leaned her head on his shoulder as they enjoyed the spectacular display of the sun setting into the pond, neither of them speaking a word. Suddenly, a spray of water jolted them out of their trance as Buddy jumped into the pond and splashed around them. They both sprang up from the dock, and Chase grabbed the dog by the collar and put his leash on.

"Okay, Mister, that's enough for one night. Sorry about that, Laney. I hope you're not too wet."

"Not at all. The cool water feels refreshing."

They headed back to the house, and their clothes were dry by the time they reached the back door. Tired from a long day, it was time for Laney to leave. She thanked Chase's mom for the lovely dinner and promised to return before she left Charleston. Marjorie gave her some apple pie to take home.

"Don't be a stranger now. Come over anytime." She hugged Laney but looked right at Chase as she spoke those words.

Chase shook his head, hoping Laney had missed his mother's lack of subtlety. Chase's dad sat in his recliner, snoring lightly, with Buddy by his side. Laney patted Buddy on the head and asked Chase to tell his dad goodbye when he woke up.

They walked out to Laney's car together, both meandering slowly before stopping to face each other.

"Thank you for tonight. I haven't had such fun in a very long time." She reached up and hugged him.

"Me too, Laney. I'm so glad you came."

They locked eyes, and for a moment, Laney thought Chase was about to kiss her. Instead, he opened the car door for her. The light from inside the car broke the veil of darkness around them. The intimate moment passed, and Laney got in the car and closed the door. Chase leaned in through the open window.

"If there's anything you need help with at the house, let me know, and I'll take care of it for you."

"Thanks, Chase, I will."

"Good night, Laney, sleep tight."

"Good night, Chase."

That night, feelings of nostalgia began to stir inside Laney. Being back in the place where she spent a lot of time as a youngster and later in her teens comforted Laney and rekindled a sense of belonging. Her friends and coworkers in New York were more like casual acquaintances, not a close-knit group one could rely on.

I didn't realize how much I missed this! Laney decided to make the most of her time in Charleston to see what might unfold.

Chapter Four

Charleston, SC – 1989

THE NEXT MORNING, LANEY went to the Main Street hardware store for cleaning supplies and a few other odds and ends after stopping at the grocery store. She wanted to clean the house from top to bottom, not only to make it livable, but also in honor of Ivy. Her grandmother took such pride in her home, and Laney wanted to respect her by making it shiny and fresh again. Dressed in jeans and a T-shirt, she added a red bandana to keep her hair out of the way. Judging from layers of dust covering everything, Laney guessed that Ivy's housekeeping efforts had slowed down in recent months.

Some of the furniture had been draped to protect it against dirt and fading. Laney removed all the covers and loaded them into the washing machine. She dug out Ivy's vacuum cleaner and spruced up the carpet and upholstery. She cleaned out the refrigerator and cupboards, then checked all the lights in the house and replaced the bulbs that were burned out. *This place is starting to look good.* Her grumbling stomach let her know it had been a while since she had eaten, so she stopped for a lunch break.

Laney wiped off the kitchen table and washed a plate and some utensils. She found napkins in the cabinet to the left of the sink, where Ivy had always kept them. She couldn't help but feel her grandmother's absence. She supposed it would take some time to adjust to the loss.

Laney ate the chicken salad she bought that morning and sipped from a bottle of iced tea when she heard something scratching at the back door. The sound continued, this time followed by whimpering. Getting up to investigate, she found Buddy on the porch with his nose pressed up against the screen door. He jumped up and started wagging his tail as if he were expecting an invitation to come inside.

"Well, hello, Buddy." Laney petted him, and he loved the attention. She surmised it wasn't his first visit to the house.

"Buddy? Buddy, where are you?" Chase called.

"He's in here with me, Chase, in the kitchen."

Chase popped his head in the back door. Buddy immediately ran to him, then lay on the floor and rolled over for a belly rub.

"I'm sorry, Laney. Ivy used to give Buddy his afternoon treats, and I guess when he sensed someone was in the house, he assumed it was okay to visit. He's still a puppy and gets a little overexuberant."

Laney laughed at the scene playing out on the floor. Chase pretended to scold the dog while Buddy clearly enjoyed their interaction.

"No need to apologize. It's nice to have a visitor."

Chase looked around and commented that the house looked good.

"Starting to look like the old house again, Lane."

"Thanks, Chase. I guess my grandmother only tended to the rooms she spent the most time in and kept the rest of the house closed up. I gave the first floor a once-over, and next I'll tackle the bedrooms upstairs."

"Buddy and I will get out of your hair, uh, or your kerchief thingy, and let you return to your chores."

She self-consciously tugged at the stray wisps of hair poking out from the bandana.

"I must look like a disaster."

"Not at all. You look great." The words left his mouth before he could stop himself, and he blushed with embarrassment. Buddy broke the awkward exchange by bolting out the back door to chase a rabbit.

"I'd better find him, or he'll run halfway to the next county."

Chase ran off after Buddy, and Laney found herself lingering in the doorway, watching him until he faded out of sight.

Laney went upstairs to clean the three bedrooms, guest bath, and Ivy's sitting room. She stripped the beds and set the linens aside to be washed. She began dusting the knick-knacks on each table and dresser, carefully replacing each one to its original location. She found all of Ivy's dresses hanging on satin-padded hangers in the closet. She decided to leave them where they were for now and donate them to the local church, along with her shoes and sweaters.

Laney started going through Ivy's chest of drawers. She felt like she was intruding on her grandmother's privacy and wasn't sure she should be doing so. Reasoning in her mind that she wasn't snooping, and it was proper for her to be tending to Ivy's belongings, she continued. She found the usual undergarments, socks, lace handkerchiefs, and such in the first drawer. In the second drawer were neatly folded shirts and a few scarves.

The bottom drawer held not clothing but cards, letters, and other papers. She started going through them and recognized some of the drawings she had made for Ivy as a young girl. She was touched that her grandmother had saved these scraps of crayon-drawn papers as keepsakes. She found nearly every card Laney had given Ivy over the years.

Beneath Laney's things was a packet of letters tied up with a rose-colored ribbon. The note on the top of the pile read, "Hank." She untied the ribbon and peeked at the first letter in the stack, dated April 1942. It was the first letter Ivy's husband Hank wrote to her while stationed overseas during World War II. Intrigued, Laney wanted to read each letter, but it was getting late.

She placed the stack of letters back where she had found them inside the drawer and closed it. However, something prevented the drawer from closing completely. She tried a second time but met with resistance once again. She pulled the drawer out completely, hoping to see what was blocking it. Crouching down to get closer, she reached to the back of the dresser and pulled out a book that had fallen behind the drawer. She opened the first page of the book and read the words, "My Diary."

Laney gasped, realizing that she held all Ivy's hopes and dreams, secrets, and innermost thoughts in her hands. She knew only snippets of Ivy's life before she was born and wanted to learn more about her grandmother as a young wife and mother. *I wonder what I will learn about my grandmother. Will there be anything about my mother in this book?* Laney would start reading it tomorrow. Right now, she needed a long, hot bath to wash away a day's worth of cleaning.

The next morning, Laney awoke to the sound of rain falling softly outside her window. Today would be a perfect day to take a break from cleaning and start reading Ivy's diary.

Hoping to learn more about her grandmother and her parents, Laney was apprehensive about what she might uncover. Much like removing the layers of dust and grime from the house, the details of her family's past needed to be uncovered.

The air held a slight chill, and Laney covered her legs with one of Ivy's crocheted afghan blankets. She took great care in handling the precious book. The pages were worn with age and starting to break away from their binding. Opening to the first entry, she began reading the story of Ivy's amazing life.

Chapter Five

Charleston, SC – 1935

A s a young girl living in Charleston, South Carolina, Ivy Spencer lacked nothing. Born in 1922, she came from an affluent family. Her father was a well-known and respected banker. Her mother ran the household, raising Ivy and her older brother Preston. A mansion by most standards, their home sat on over twenty-five acres, complete with a reflecting pool, numerous gardens, servants' quarters, and horse stables.

Ivy was enrolled in the finest school. She attended Cotillion at the age of fourteen and was taught proper etiquette and manners. Despite her many advantages, Ivy yearned for the one thing absent from her life—affection. Her parents were not demonstrative and seldom showed their feelings. Starved for physical contact, Ivy longed to be hugged or caressed. Her mother believed that coddling children made them weak and insisted they learn to be self-sufficient. She never considered that young girls might become stronger and more confident with a deep sense of belonging, caring, and love. As a consequence, feelings of inadequacy plagued Ivy throughout her life. She adopted a cool demeanor to mask the pain of emotional neglect in her youth.

April 5, 1935

Dear Diary,

I try so hard to please mother, but nothing I do meets with her approval. I fear I'm not as strong as she wishes me to be and fall short of her expectations. Sometimes, I imagine her holding me when I'm scared instead of telling me to be brave. I'm not brave.

Throughout her teenage years, Ivy attended an all-girl finishing school and lived in a dormitory. She kept to herself most of the time, hiding her timidity and lack of social skills. The other girls misconstrued her behavior as aloofness and thought Ivy to be a rich snob. They avoided her for the most part; thus, she made no friends at school. Upon returning home after graduation, her family considered Ivy the perfect age for marriage and arranged a meeting with the son of one of her father's business associates.

At twenty-four years of age, Henry Westfield's future was predetermined; he would carry on the family tradition and become a banker. Henry—Hank to family and friends—worked hard to meet his father's expectations. He spent long days at the bank and attended business functions in the evenings. His good looks, impeccable manners, and decorum established him as one of Charleston's most eligible bachelors, with several young ladies vying for his attention. Although flattered, Hank knew enough to recognize that they were more attracted to his place in society than to him.

May 12, 1939

Dear Diary,

I'm happy to be done with school. I prayed that after graduating, mother would welcome me home with open arms. That was not to be the case. Instead, I find myself being matched with a man whom I've never met. He is older than me, and I doubt we will have much in common. My misery continues.

Ivy and Hank were introduced to each other at a dinner party attended by both their parents and her brother Preston. Her first impression of Henry Westfield was that, although handsome, he appeared formal and stilted. Perhaps she misinterpreted his politeness as being standoffish, much like her classmates misjudged her at school. She wondered if there was more to Hank Westfield beneath his reserved exterior.

The five-course meal was served outside beneath a grape-vined pergola. Fragrant hydrangeas, irises, and a variety of bushes and shrubs filled the air with a sweet aroma. The early spring evening was comfortably cool, well ahead of the stifling Southern humidity and annoying June bugs of summer.

After dinner, Ivy's mother suggested that she and Hank take a stroll. Ivy complied and led Hank to the walking path that encircled the estate. Avoiding Hank's gaze, Ivy tried to conceal her awkwardness. After a long, uncomfortable silence, Hank initiated conversation with comments about the lovely weather and how much he enjoyed dinner. Ivy responded with only a polite, "Thank you." Hank had his work cut out for him if he wanted to break the ice.

Although she barely looked up, Ivy's breathtaking beauty did not escape Hank. Her striking brown eyes, slender figure, and lilting voice were quite attractive to him. As they walked along the path, Hank continued to make small talk, hoping to draw Ivy out of her shell.

"Tell me, did you have any favorite courses in school?"

"Not really. We studied the usual math, English, and science. And of course, the mandatory classes for girls, such as home economics, sewing, and fine arts."

"Sounds like a well-rounded education."

"I suppose."

"You don't sound satisfied with your schooling."

"To be honest, I hated being away from home. I didn't have many friends and spent most of my time alone. I liked a few of my instructors, though, which made my time there bearable."

Ivy stared into space sorrowfully, thinking about school. She looked sad, and Hank feared he had brought up a painful subject for her. He skillfully diverted to a more pleasant topic.

"What kind of music do you enjoy, Ivy?"

"I enjoy swing and jazz, but don't get to listen to them as often as I would like. Mother prefers Bach and Beethoven, while I like Benny Goodman."

"Me too! I hear his band may be coming to Charleston soon. I'd love to take you to see them."

"That would be delightful, Hank."

Hank considered it a victory when Ivy willingly shared her thoughts and feelings with him. She was unlike most of the women he met, who wanted merely to attach themselves to him for the promise of financial stability. Ivy seemed genuine and sincere, and Hank wanted to know more about this interesting young girl. To his surprise, she kept the conversation going.

"Where did you go to school?" Ivy asked Hank.

"My father enrolled me at the University of South Carolina, where I studied banking."

"Did you like it?"

"Yes, I did. It was fascinating to learn about business and financial strategies, especially after the impact of the Great Depression."

"I'm afraid I don't understand much about that. My parents didn't teach me anything about money or economics."

"I guess it's in my blood."

After becoming a little more acquainted with Hank, Ivy found herself attracted to him. Handsome and debonair, he made her feel at ease. She never opened up to anyone as she had with Hank. Before long, though, the familiar feelings of insecurity and inadequacy crept into her thoughts. She wondered why he would consider marrying someone with so little to offer as a wife.

Dusk began to fall, casting an orange hue across the sky. Fearing darkness would be upon them soon, Ivy suggested they return to the house. Hank agreed, although he enjoyed being alone with Ivy under the magical glow of the setting sun. "Thank you, Miss Ivy, for the lovely dinner and walk. I hope we can meet again soon."

Ivy's parents stared at her, waiting for her response. Her cheeks flushed, and she quietly replied, "Thank you, I would like that."

May 15, 1939

Dear Diary,

Tonight I met Henry Westfield. At Mother's insistence, we strolled through the gardens to get acquainted. He is sophisticated, holds a respectable banking job, and is articulate. Overcome by my shyness, I contributed little to the conversation. I don't think he found me the least bit attractive or interesting.

Surely this will be one more disappointment for Mother as she had optimistically hoped we would wed.

After their first meeting, Hank often called on Ivy. They dated regularly for the next few months, attending garden parties, business affairs, and family gatherings together. Hank loved everything about Ivy. Poised and proper in social situations, she was tender and kindhearted among family and friends. She had a vulnerability about her that made him want to protect and care for her forever. He knew what he wanted and would waste no more time. He would ask Ivy Spencer to be his wife, and hoped that she would accept his marriage proposal.

Ivy enjoyed spending these past months with Hank. They talked about anything and everything. He was sweet and kind, a gentleman at all times, and treated her like a lady. Ivy's inhibitions and insecurities disappeared whenever they were together.

For their date one evening, Ivy selected a pale pink dress and matching shoes. She arranged her hair in an updo, adding an ivory clip with small pearls. Pleased with her appearance, she waited for Hank to arrive.

Hank selected his best tailored suit and slipped the engagement ring he had purchased for Ivy in the breast pocket. Tonight was a big step in his life, and his nerves were on edge. Ivy looked beautiful, and he complimented her on her dress as he escorted her to the car.

"Hank, we've been driving for almost an hour. Where are we going this evening?"

"I'm taking you to a quaint little restaurant I learned about from a colleague of mine. It's not too much farther. It will be worth the drive, I promise."

The valet at Oscar's opened the door for Ivy and led her to the covered portico. Hank came around the back of the car to join her, took her arm, and they walked into the restaurant. He gave the maître d' his name, and they were shown to a private table marked "reserved." The opulent furnishings and antebellum décor were quite impressive. Glowing candles on each table and a roaming violinist added to the room's romantic atmosphere. Hank ordered a bottle of red wine to start their evening.

"Hank, this restaurant is beautiful. I had no idea you were taking me to such a fancy place."

Hank reached for Ivy's hand and pressed it in his. "Nothing outshines your beauty, Ivy."

Ivy gazed into Hank's eyes. His words, the music, and the wine were all affecting her. "Thank you, Hank. You always know the right thing to say."

They dined on fresh lobster with all the trimmings and coconut cream pie for dessert. The waiter cleared the table, and Hank couldn't wait another minute. He knelt beside Ivy, out of view from the other diners. Startled, Ivy looked at him, not knowing what was happening.

"Ivy, I fell in love with you the first time we met at your parents' house. You are the most fascinating, amazing woman I've ever known. I want to spend the rest of my life with you. Will you do me the honor of marrying me and being my wife?"

"Oh, Hank! This is so sudden. I wasn't expecting this. I don't know what to say."

"Say yes and be my bride."

"Yes, yes, I will marry you, Hank."

He slipped the ring on Ivy's finger and gently kissed her lips. Embarrassed about showing affection in a public restaurant, Ivy kissed him quickly. She looked down at her hand to admire the engagement ring.

"Do you like it, Ivy? If not, we can exchange it for another."

"It's perfect, Hank, just like you."

August 12, 1939

Dear Diary,

This evening Hank took me to dinner and proposed marriage on bended knee. He placed the most beautiful ring on my finger and asked me to be his bride. I accepted, knowing in my heart that he is the only man I will ever love. I hope and pray I can be a suitable wife. I suppose time will tell. The news should please mother and father. I will tell them tomorrow.

Chapter Six

Charleston, SC – 1989

ENTHRALLED BY THE STORY unfolding at her fingertips, Laney lost track of time. Having missed lunch, she read until early evening. She hated to tear herself away from the detailed account of Ivy's life: the pain and joy, sorrow and happiness that she had experienced. Laney had known Ivy as a strong, independent grandmother who had raised her from the age of four. She had never imagined Ivy as an insecure teenager and young wife before finding her inner strength and maturing into a formidable woman. Learning this made Laney love and admire her grandmother more and miss her with greater intensity.

Laney thought about the letter once again. The unexpected revelation of learning that her father was alive, at least until Laney was eight years old, unsettled her. *What does this all mean, and how do I make sense of this?*

She went downstairs to the kitchen for something to eat when the telephone rang. Chase's voice on the other end was a welcome break.

"Hey, Lane, how's it going?"

"Okay, Chase. I've been reading all afternoon."

"Something good, I hope."

"Yesterday I found my grandmother's diary in one of her dressers while cleaning her bedroom. I started reading it and have learned many new things. Also, her lawyer gave me a letter she wrote to me. It held disturbing information that I'm trying to sort through."

"Do you want to talk about it? I'd be happy to listen."

"That would be nice, Chase. I haven't had dinner yet, have you?"

"Not yet. I can pick up a pizza and come over for a while."

"A pizza sounds perfect," said Laney, grateful she wouldn't have to cook tonight.

"See you in about half an hour."

Still in her pajamas, Laney had enough time for a quick shower and to dress before Chase arrived.

When they were through eating dinner, Chase said to Laney, "Tell me what's bothering you, Lane."

Laney smiled at him. From the time they were kids, she had confided in him. "You could always read me like a book, Chase."

"Still can. What's wrong?"

"The day I met with the lawyer for the reading of my grandmother's will, he gave me a letter from her. She wrote it a while back with instructions to give it to me after her passing. It contains startling information about my father. I realize it was a long time ago, but do you remember when I was about eight years old, I told you I thought I saw a man who looked like my father?"

Chase thought for a moment and then recalled the incident. "Yes, you said something about being afraid to go home and hung out at my house for the afternoon."

"That's right. Your mom was so nice and let me help bake cookies to keep me occupied. According to the letter from Ivy, the man I saw that day was my father."

Laney's voice cracked, and her hands started to shake. Chase scooted closer to comfort her. He put his arm around her, and she nestled into him. "Do you want to tell me what the letter said?"

Laney told him everything that Ivy wrote in the letter. She recounted how her father came back after several years to extort money from Ivy, how Preston stepped in to make sure Peter never returned to bother them, and how Ivy kept it all from Laney.

It took Chase a minute or two to digest all this information. He didn't know the right thing to say, so he waited for Laney to speak again.

"He was alive, and my grandmother didn't tell me. I should be terribly upset with her for keeping this secret, but she was protecting me. I remember being scared to death that he would hurt my mom or me." Laney began to cry, and Chase held her closer. She had been holding back so many emotions this past week—Ivy's death, the will, the letter, the diary, being back home, and seeing Chase again.

"It's okay," Chase said, consoling her. "Let it out, Laney."

"What upsets me the most is that my grandmother agonized for years with her decision to keep my father from me—always questioning whether it was the right thing to do."

"That shows how much she cared about you."

"Yes, she did, and I realize how deeply she loved me."

Curious, Chase asked her, "Ivy said she never saw your father again, right?"

"Yes, that's correct. Why do you ask?"

"I wonder what happened to him. Do you think Preston killed him?"

Laney hadn't thought about that. "I guess it's possible. My grandmother said Uncle Preston was a changed man after returning home from the war.

"Changed in what way?"

"He told her that witnessing atrocities against women and children at the hands of enemy soldiers infuriated him. His experiences made him aggressive towards bullies and very protective of her and my mother."

"Is he still alive?"

"No, he passed away several years ago. There has to be another way to find out what happened to my father."

Unsure how to uncover the details surrounding Peter Armstrong's disappearance, Chase promised to give it some thought. "Let me see what I can come up with. For now, though, I think you've had enough for one day."

Laney appreciated his protectiveness and concern for her. "You're right, Chase. It's been a long day, and I'm worn out."

Chase got up from the sofa to leave. Standing together in the doorway, Laney hugged him. "Thanks for being here and helping me sort through all this."

He hugged her, softly rubbing her back. "You don't have to thank me, Lane. I'm always here for you."

Laney felt his arms around her, his breath on her neck, and the closeness of his body pressed against hers. She sensed a change in their relationship. *Is Chase's "big brother" role transforming into something more?*

Chase kissed the top of her head and told Laney to get a good night's sleep. "I'll call you tomorrow to check in on you."

Exhausted, Laney went right to bed but tossed and turned all night. She checked the clock on her nightstand, certain it must be time to get up. To her dismay, it was only 1:30; she had only been asleep for about two and a half hours. Giving up the futile attempt to sleep, she turned on the light and decided to read some more pages of Ivy's diary.

Charleston, SC – 1940

On Saturday, April 6, 1940, the wedding of Hank and Ivy was the talk of Charleston. Several hundred people attended, predominantly friends and acquaintances of their parents, only a few of whom Ivy knew. Being the center of attention intimidated her, and she struggled to maintain her composure. Accustomed to interacting with large groups of businessmen and associates, Hank took it in stride and handled himself expertly.

Ivy wore the wedding gown her mother selected for her. Imported Irish lace and pearls surrounded the high neckline of the chiffon dress. The delicate fabric flowed elegantly over Ivy's slender body. She styled her long hair high atop her head with tender ringlets framing her face and the back of her neck. Ivy donned a simple veil with matching lace around the fingertip-length edges.

Her mother helped her dress and adjusted her gown and headdress. Ivy looked like a model in a fashion magazine. Offering little advice for Ivy on her wedding day, her mother told her to be a good wife, to respect and honor her husband, and to run a smooth household. Ivy hoped for more on such a momentous occasion, but as usual, her mother displayed no emotion. There were no reassuring hugs or caresses to calm her nerves. It felt more like a business transaction, with her mother handing her over to her new husband.

"There now," her mother said matter-of-factly as she smoothed an imaginary wrinkle from Ivy's gown, "you're ready to be Mrs. Henry Westfield."

Hank's brother James served as his best man, and Ivy's second cousin Elisabeth witnessed the ceremony as matron of honor. As the traditional wedding march resounded through the main chapel of St. Augustine's Church, Ivy took the arm of her father and proceeded down the long, white-carpeted aisle. Onlookers gawked at her as she passed them, clearly taken by her exquisite beauty and grace.

The wedding guests faded into the background as Ivy directed her attention solely toward her intended, who waited at the altar. Ivy's father lifted her veil with care, kissed her on the cheek, and placed her hand in Hank's. He looked adoringly into Ivy's eyes, captivated by her beauty. He clasped her trembling hands, and they turned to face the priest to begin the ceremony.

They spoke their vows to each other as if they were the only two people in the church. Hank slid the matching band to Ivy's diamond engagement ring on her finger; she placed a simple gold band on his. As the priest declared, "I now pronounce you husband and wife," Hank turned to Ivy and kissed her lips. Ivy's knees began to buckle. Without missing a step, Hank swooped her into his arms to save her from an embarrassing tumble in front of the congregation. At that moment, Ivy knew Hank would always be there to love and protect her.

The wedding dinner was held at the High Mont Country Club since both the Westfields and the Spencers had been members for decades. Champagne flowed freely as their guests dined on filet mignon. All eyes were on her throughout the evening. Hank, sensing Ivy's embarrassment, never once left her side.

Dancing together for the first time as a married couple, Hank and Ivy glided gracefully across the floor. Ivy began to relax and enjoy the reception with her new husband. They had eyes only for each other as they cut their five-tiered wedding cake. Keeping with tradition, they fed each other a piece of cake for luck, then clinked their champagne glasses together in a toast to a lifetime of love and happiness.

Hank led his bride to the car and driver, waiting just outside the reception hall. They were whisked away to the honeymoon suite of the Charleston Inn to start their life together as husband and wife.

The stress and excitement of the long day caught up with Ivy, and she was overcome with exhaustion. Still, she was determined to fulfill Hank's wedding night expectations. She excused herself to the bathroom and removed her wedding gown, carefully hanging it up on the satin-covered hanger in the closet. She washed her face and donned a white silk peignoir and slippers.

Captivated by her beauty, Hank gazed at Ivy as she stood in the doorway, bathed in candlelight. Ivy walked to her side of the bed and slipped between the sheets. Trembling in anticipation of what was about to happen, she couldn't look at him.

"Ivy, I understand you're nervous and a little scared, but I want you to know that I would never hurt you. Tonight is our wedding night, but we will be married for a very long time, and there is no need to rush. You're tired and need your rest. Sleep, my darling, and dream of our life together and all the good things that await us."

Ivy was incredulous! She had all she ever wanted—a loving husband who adored and cared for her, attentive to her needs. She didn't want to tempt fate by trying to figure out why she'd been so fortunate. Feeling safe and warm in Hank's arms, she did exactly as he said.

When Ivy's breath became soft and even, Hank kissed her cheek, pulled the cover over her shoulders, and held her in his arms until the bright light of day streaked through their bedroom window.

April 10, 1940

Dear Diary,

Suddenly, my life feels like a fairy tale. Hank is so caring and more than I could have imagined in a husband. This must be the true love I have always heard about. He is sweet, gentle, and patient with me. He makes me feel special and fills a void I've had since I was a child, starved for affection from Mother and Father. Please, dear Lord, don't ever take my darling Hank away from me.

Chapter Seven

Hank and Ivy temporarily settled into the guest house on Ivy's parents' estate until they found a home of their own. Their first few weeks of marriage were spent learning each other's habits and routines. Ivy appreciated Hank's patience in the bedroom but realized that sooner or later, they would make love. She wanted to be intimate with him but was unsure of what to do. Her mother's reticence in discussing the subject left Ivy ill-prepared.

Knowing she'd never been with a man before, Hank took great care to be gentle and considerate of Ivy's inhibitions. Although he hadn't been with a great many women, he knew that making love to Ivy would be different. He'd never been in love with or cared for a woman as deeply as Ivy.

Preparing for bed, Ivy sat at her vanity brushing her hair in her nightgown. The sight of her filled Hank with desire. Without uttering a word, he took her hand and led her to their bed. He kissed her forehead, her cheek, and then her lips, igniting a passion inside him. Ivy kissed him back with fervor.

Hank's movements sent a tingling sensation through Ivy's body like a shockwave. She had never felt like this before and slowly relaxed under his skillful touch. It was not only the act of their lovemaking that thrilled her, but also the intensity of their emotional union. She loved Hank more than anything, and he felt the same way about her. This physical connection only deepened their love and brought them closer together.

April 20, 1940

Dear Diary,

Having no experience in the intimate relations between a man and a woman, I fear I'm inadequate. Even now, on these pages which contain only my private thoughts, I'm not able to describe how it feels to be with my husband in this way. I can only write that my life continues to exceed my expectations for happiness. From the little I know about such things, I believe it is now possible for me to be in a family way. It is almost too much to hope for.

While driving into Charleston one day, Hank turned off the main road onto a small country back road. Surprised by the detour, Ivy asked him why he had turned.

"I think I may have found us a home, Ivy."

"Really?"

"Yes. One of my colleagues at the bank told me about a house that's in the process of foreclosure. The owners lost their money when their debts became insurmountable. They couldn't afford to live in the house and were forced to abandon it."

"That's so sad," lamented Ivy, thinking about a family walking away from their home.

"I agree, but the effects of the Great Depression are still being felt by many."

Hank turned the car onto Cypress Lane and stopped in front of the ornate gate with the numbers 5037 engraved in the wrought-iron scrollwork. Judging from the size and architecture of the house, the previous owners had, at one time been quite wealthy.

The white two-story, Queen Anne–style home was built just after the turn of the century in 1904. Positioned at the far-left side of the house, the front door sat adjacent to polygonal tower-shaped rooms extending from the first to the second floor. The expansive front porch wrapped around to the kitchen door toward the back on the right side of the house. White spindles flanked each side of the extra-wide stairway, creating an inviting entrance. Ornate, filigreed spandrels and cornices decorated each section of the porch and upstairs balcony outside the master bedroom. Blue hydrangea bushes at the base of the porch made an impressive display of color and beauty.

The massive oak front door featured swirled etched glass, matching the twin sidelight windows. Upon entering the house, an impressive L-shaped staircase leading to the second floor occupied the space beyond the foyer. Halfway up the stairs, three large stained-glass windows brought in light from the south-facing rear of the house.

Each room had its own sense of charm and sophistication. The first floor had a parlor, a formal dining room, a kitchen, and a small, round sitting room that faced the driveway in front of the house. The kitchen had a butler's pantry lined with shelves on three sides. Upstairs were three bedrooms, another sitting room, and a good-sized bathroom. The main rooms each had their own fireplace.

The house, over thirty-five years old, was in remarkable condition. It boasted modern conveniences such as hot and cold running water, wainscoting in the dining room, and decorative ceramic tiles in the bathroom and kitchen. The immediate grounds around the house had a pond, several mature oak and cypress trees, and a vegetable garden. The fifty-acre estate sat on a long, winding road with only one or two other houses nearby.

"What do you think, Ivy?"

The house possessed a homelike quality Ivy admired, and she easily envisioned herself living here and raising a family. "Oh, Hank, it's beautiful, but I fear it is beyond our means."

"Not at all. In fact, I already bought it. The potential investment return is too good to pass up."

"Hank Westfield, you didn't!"

Ivy's reaction, a combination of surprise, fear, and amazement all rolled into one, caught Hank off guard. Her eyes began to fill with tears. Hank feared he'd made a mistake by purchasing the house without talking to her first. Accustomed to making his own decisions, Hank hadn't considered discussing it with his wife. He realized he had a lot to learn about being a husband.

"Ivy, my darling, what's wrong? I thought for sure you would love this house as much as I do. Are you not pleased?"

"It's not that, Hank. On the contrary. But the house is so big, and I'm afraid I can't take care of it myself. We had servants, and I never learned how to cook or clean a home."

Hank gently wiped her tears with a linen handkerchief from his coat pocket. "Ivy, perhaps you didn't realize that I make a handsome salary at the bank, and having enough money is not a concern for us. I fully intend to see to it that you have all the help you need to run a household."

Ivy clung so closely to Hank that he felt the pounding of her heart through her coat. She didn't know whether to cry or shout out loud in sheer happiness. In these hard times, she and

Hank were fortunate enough to afford this beautiful home. Filled with gratitude, Ivy said a silent prayer of thanks.

"I love you, Hank. You've made me so happy!"

The Westfields gathered their belongings from the guest house and moved into their new home on Cypress Lane in early 1940. It didn't take long for Ivy and Hank to furnish and decorate the home to their liking. Ivy designated the bedroom next to the master suite as a nursery. She looked forward to having a little one in the bassinet as soon as the good Lord sent them their first child.

Ivy refused Hank's offer to hire a maid, at least for the time being. Determined to be independent and self-sufficient, she dedicated herself to learning how to manage a household. Teaching herself how to cook by trial and error, she cleaned the house and revitalized the abandoned garden, even growing her own vegetables.

May 15, 1940

Dear Diary,

Hank and I purchased our first home. While I'm appreciative of the hospitality afforded us by my parents, it is much more enjoyable to be under our own roof. I found great delight in selecting our furnishings and decorating each room. I look forward to hosting dinners, birthday parties for our children, and creating a lifetime of happy memories inside these walls. All who enter our door will find joy and happiness abound.

Chapter Eight

Charleston, SC – 1940

SETTLING INTO HER NEW life on Cypress Lane, Ivy enjoyed birdwatching from her favorite rattan chaise lounge on the front porch. Sparrows and painted buntings flitted through the trees. Great blue herons waded in the pond. These magnificent birds sat motionless for long periods, searching for their prey beneath the shimmering water. Ivy often caught a glimpse of a heron striking quickly to snatch a small fish or frog to eat for lunch.

Intruding on the serenity of their peaceful country life was the weekly radio broadcast by President Roosevelt. During his Fireside Chat on a late Sunday in May 1940, the president talked about the tragic events happening overseas. He urged every American to contribute whatever they could to their local Red Cross chapter in support of their cause. He reminded the nation that the United States was strong and prepared for war, even though some thought otherwise.

Closer to home in Charleston, the Navy Yard, which manufactured and repaired ships at the docks on the Cooper River, began increasing its workforce to meet the new demands. Ivy did her part by donating items to the Red Cross in town and asked both her parents and Hank's parents to contribute as well.

The newspaper and radio reports grew more bleak each day. Whenever Hank's father came to visit, the conversation inevitably turned to events happening across the globe.

"Did you hear that Germany invaded Denmark and Norway?"

"Yes, Father, I read that in the paper today, along with news that Italy entered the war by invading southern France," Hank answered.

"President Roosevelt said it best in his commencement speech at the University of Virginia. He told the graduating class, "On this tenth day of June 1940, the hand that held the dagger has struck it into the back of its neighbor.""

"I'm afraid it's only a matter of time until we get involved."

Whenever Hank and his father discussed the war, Ivy retreated to the tranquility of the backyard to avoid listening to talk of the tension brewing on the other side of the world. Nothing frightened Ivy more than the thought of war.

To increase the military, President Roosevelt enacted the first peacetime conscription in United States history on September 16, 1940. All men between the ages of twenty-one and forty-five were required to register for the draft. Of those registered, 900,000 would be inducted into training. Those selected from the draft lottery would serve at least one year in the armed forces. Both James and Preston had already enlisted. Hank signed up for the draft, and thankfully, his number was not drawn in the first lottery. Still, Hank and Ivy lived in fear that soon he would be called to serve his country.

September 16, 1940

Dear Diary,

The newness and excitement of owning our first home together has been diminished by the threat of an impending war. The world, as we have come to know it, is changing rapidly, and I'm hard-pressed to adjust to it. Hank signed up as required of him. I know I must be brave, but I think only of my husband and our future. I fear my newfound happiness, which has eluded me my whole life, will be fleeting, at best.

Ivy had become quite a capable homemaker and cook. She had an innate knack for adding spices and flavors to enhance her dishes. Her delicious meals produced mouthwatering scents, which wafted throughout the house. After several attempts, she had perfected a scrumptious apple pie, complete with cutout heart shapes on top. With her new skills, Ivy and Hank planned to host Thanksgiving for both their families.

Preston, attending basic training at Camp Croft in nearby Spartanburg, couldn't come home for the holiday. James, stationed at Camp Livingston in Alexandria, Louisiana, wrote to Hank saying he wouldn't be able to get leave for Thanksgiving but would try to be home for Christmas.

Ivy set the elegant table with an imported linen tablecloth and napkin set she had received as a wedding gift from one of Hank's aunts. She added tall, white tapers to each end of the table. For the centerpiece, she arranged a vase of camellias that Hank had surprised her with earlier that morning.

"These could never be as lovely as you are, but I want you to have them to adorn your beautiful table."

Ivy kissed Hank on the cheek and thanked him for his thoughtfulness. She was so happy that he understood the importance of hosting her first dinner party for their family. As their guests began to arrive, Hank greeted them at the door, welcoming them into their home.

Nervous and jittery, Ivy hoped everything would go well and meet with her mother's approval. She needn't have worried; dinner was a smashing success, and everyone raved about her tasty apple pie. To her delight, her mother, in her own stilted way, was most complimentary.

"Your expertise in hosting a dinner party amazes me, Ivy," her mother told her. "I'm not surprised by your capabilities, but by the fact that you learned how to do all this on your own. I fear I didn't do enough to prepare you for domesticity and am pleased you have flourished, despite my maternal shortcomings."

Her mother's declaration of inadequacy in raising a daughter shocked Ivy. She had never heard her say anything as self-deprecating as this. Ivy saw her mother differently, approachable and endearing.

"You taught me grace, dignity, and how to put my best foot forward. You enabled me to think for myself. These were far more valuable lessons than how to make a pie."

It was her mother's turn to see her daughter in a new light, and a transformation occurred in their relationship, each woman appreciating the other's virtues with mutual respect. Ivy couldn't have been more appreciative on this day of thanks, and hugged her mother. Quite out of character, her mother reciprocated with equal intensity.

After their guests departed, Hank helped Ivy with the dishes.

"That was without a doubt the best Thanksgiving dinner I ever ate," exclaimed Hank as he hugged his wife, lifted her off the ground, and twirled her in a circle. "It was a meal fit for a king!"

"I'm so happy you enjoyed it. I hope it will be one of many special dinners we share with our families in our home."

"I'm sure it will be, my love," he told her, hugging her again, noticing Ivy seemed a bit rounder in the middle.

Thursday, November 28, 1940

Dear Diary,

Hosting my first holiday dinner exceeded my expectations. I'm most thankful for the change in the relationship between Mother and me. We have reached a turning point where she no longer considers me to be a child or awkward adolescent, but a mature woman running my own household. I admit to being stunned by her display of affection and recognition, but happy that we've arrived at this point. Hank was quite pleased with our dinner and told me so after our guests went home. I noticed a strange look in his eyes when he held me in his arms; it's as if he knows something I do not. I'm exhausted from today's events and will end here. Good night.

The December evenings grew cooler, bringing a noticeable crispness into the air. The first batch of Christmas cookies was cooling on a wire rack when Ivy heard a frantic knock at the front door. She ran to the foyer and opened the door wide. A beautiful Frasier Fir, emanating a fresh pine scent, filled the entire doorway. She couldn't see who was holding up the tree because its thick trunk and full branches blocked her view.

"Ho, ho, ho!" Hank sang out merrily.

Laughing at his playful tone, she joined in the gaiety and asked, "Santa, is that you?"

Hank came around to the front of the tree. "Isn't she a beauty?"

"Where shall we put it?" Ivy asked.

"I think the best spot will be in front of the windows in the parlor. The ceiling is tall, and we'll be able to see the lights from outside." He positioned the tree with the best branches facing the middle of the room. "I picked up some lights and ornaments at the five-and-dime so we can decorate it together."

In her excitement over adorning the tree, Ivy spun around joyously. She became dizzy and unsteady on her feet. Lurching toward her, Hank quickly grabbed Ivy and led her to the sofa.

"Ivy, what is it? Are you not feeling well? Let me get you a glass of water."

"I'll be okay. I've been getting these dizzy spells on and off recently, and some of my dresses fit a little tight."

Ivy didn't make the connection and thought perhaps her newly acquired love for cooking had added a few extra pounds. Hank knew the cause right away and knelt beside her.

"I believe you and I are going to be parents," he said softly.

Astonished, Ivy asked him, "Are you sure? How do you know this?"

Hank smiled sweetly. "You've had a glow in your cheeks and a gleam in your eyes for a few months, but I really began to notice right after Thanksgiving."

"With the news of the war and the holidays, I didn't take notice that I had missed my courses. Are you pleased?" she asked, hopeful that he shared her excitement.

"Of course I am, my love," Hank reassured her. "Our little family is growing!"

December 18, 1940

Dear Diary,

I'm in a family way. I suffered from several weeks of nausea, followed by a steady swelling of my midsection. We celebrated an extra joyous holiday this year, knowing that a little one would soon be added to our family. Hank promised to start making plans for a nursery right after the New Year, and I will start sewing baby clothes. Everything is perfect, and I hope it always stays this way!

Chapter Nine

Charleston, SC – 1941

O N MARCH 27, 1941, Lillian Augusta Westfield made her grand entrance into the world. Hank and Ivy were immediately infatuated with this little pink bundle of love, who they called Lily. Since Ivy had a difficult delivery and required bed rest for a few weeks, Hank hired a nanny to care for both the baby and Lily.

Caroline Parker was the daughter of Hank's childhood nanny, and the two of them had grown up together. She welcomed the opportunity to continue her family's tradition of caring for the Westfield children. While grateful for the help, Ivy wanted to care for Lily as much as possible. Caroline often included Ivy in Lily's bathing and feeding, and they formed a harmonious relationship from the start.

April 2, 1941

Dear Diary,

God has sent us a child whom I hope will be the first of many. Our daughter Lillian's birth produced quite a bit of pain, but all was forgotten the first time I held her in my arms. She is sweet and pure perfection. Although my foray into motherhood is just beginning, the love I feel for Lily is already abundantly more than I have received in a lifetime from my own mother. And so, my life as a mother begins.

Each night after work, Hank went directly to the nursery to visit Lily. She wrapped her tender little fingers around his as he held her in his arms, gingerly supporting her head. He never felt so attached to another human being, and he adored his precious daughter. Hank, Ivy, and Lily sat for hours on the bed cooing and cuddling together.

"Ivy, my darling, motherhood agrees with you." He stared into her eyes and continued, "You're absolutely radiant, and your eyes sparkle with the same intensity as the stars on a moonlit night. I know it is too soon to discuss, but I hope we have a houseful of children together!"

"Me too, my love!" Tears spilled from Ivy's eyes at their shared sentiment.

June 1941 brought several milestones into Hank and Ivy's lives. They celebrated their one-year wedding anniversary. At three months old, Lily started holding her head up by herself. Hank liked to shake Lily's rattle and watch her grab it with her tiny fingers.

The early summer season blossomed with a variety of flowers blooming around the house. Azalea bushes put on a spectacular pink and white display. The huge Magnolia tree near the pond was full of creamy-white flowers, which permeated the air with their lemony-citrus scent. Ivy kept the kitchen windows open to let the fragrance fill the house. The hydrangea bushes were also in bloom with their pom-pom-like, blue-petaled flowers. Ivy snipped a few of the flower heads and placed them in a vase to make a centerpiece for the dining room table.

One day, Ivy answered a knock at the front door. There stood a woman, close in age to Ivy, with a homemade pie in her hand.

"Hello! My name is Helen Buchanan, and I'm your neighbor."

Ivy returned the introduction, "Hello, Helen, I'm Ivy Westfield. It's so nice to meet you. Won't you please come in?"

Ivy made a pot of tea, and the two women became acquainted. Later, Helen introduced her husband, Ben, to Hank, and they shared their talents and hobbies with each other. Ben taught Hank about farming and gardening, and Hank educated Ben about banking and stocks. The

Buchanans had one son named Joseph, who was about a year older than Lily. The two couples had a lot in common and spent so much time together that they considered themselves family.

News of the impending threat of war often interrupted day-to-day life. Although the president claimed the United States was not closer to getting involved, Hank and his father surmised the U.S. would join forces with Britain against Hitler. Hank sensed Ivy's growing trepidation and offered to take her out for the evening to get her mind off it.

"What would you say to a night out? We can see that new movie you've been talking about, *Here Comes Mr. Jordan*, with Robert Montgomery."

"That sounds wonderful!"

Although Ivy enjoyed spending time with Lily, she appreciated the chance to spend an evening alone with her husband. She bathed in her favorite lavender-scented bubble bath, then applied a slight touch of rouge to her cheeks and the red lipstick on her lips that Hank liked so well. She selected a light, sleeveless cotton dress to stay cool while in the theater and had high hopes for a relaxing and romantic night on the town.

They arrived at the Gloria Theater on King Street. Hank bought two tickets, and they chose their seats. As the curtain opened, Ivy waited for the movie to begin. Instead, the newsreel preceded the film, showing graphic scenes from the fighting overseas. For the first time, Ivy saw actual footage of

President Roosevelt instead of only hearing his voice on the radio. Disturbing images of battleships, tanks, and burning airplanes spiraling into the ocean were too much for her to bear. She closed her eyes and covered her ears, trying to shut out the sounds and scenes before her—images certain to linger long after the lights came up.

Hank slipped his arm around Ivy, and she buried her face against his chest to block the screen. At last, the newsreel ended, and the opening credits of the film began to roll. Ivy tried to steady herself and turn her attention back to the movie, but the knot in her stomach refused to loosen.

She leaned closer to Hank and whispered, "Hank, I don't think I can sit through the picture after that. Could we go home?"

Hank looked down at her, concern softening his voice. "Of course. I should've thought about the newsreel." He gave her shoulder a reassuring squeeze. "Come on. Let's get you out of here."

Sleep eluded Ivy that night. She envisioned Hank in an army uniform, leaving home to fight the war in an unknown land. She couldn't bear the thought of him being on the other side of the globe without any contact, not knowing if he was safe or engaged in a bloody battle. She broke out in a cold sweat at the thought of him being wounded... or worse.

Lily's crying interrupted her thoughts, and she welcomed the diversion. Caroline was getting ready to feed the baby.

"Please, Caroline, let me give Lily her bottle tonight," Ivy begged her. Hearing the desperation in her voice, Caroline placed the baby in Ivy's arms and left them alone. She hoped Ivy would find solace in caring for Lily.

Hank awoke and found himself alone in the four-poster bed, wondering where Ivy had gone. He crept quietly into the nursery. Bathed in the moonlight filtering through the window, he spied Ivy sitting in the rocking chair, softly singing to a sleepy Lily. He stopped for a moment to capture the image of the two most important people in his life, as if to engrave it in his mind for eternity. Ivy placed Lily back in her crib, and they returned to their room, sleeping in each other's arms, clinging to one another.

July 23, 1941

Dear Diary,

My fears are rising as we are bombarded by news of the war overseas. Every day, the threat of danger creeps closer to home. Hank tries to lift my spirits and waylay my fears, but there is no escaping the events, not even at the picture show. I love him and Lily more than anything and pray our little family remains safe.

In November 1941, Lily turned eight months old. She slept through the night and spent more time awake during the day. She started babbling and giggling at the sound of her own voice. The afternoons were getting chilly, and Ivy bundled Lily in a sweater while strolling through the yard with the baby in her pram. The mighty oak tree put on a brilliant display of color in the last weeks of fall. Dazzling oranges and reds were reflected in the still water of the pond, creating a stunning portrait of nature's beauty. Soon, the magnificent tree would drop its leaves and lie dormant for the winter.

That year, President Roosevelt changed the date of Thanksgiving back to the fourth Thursday in November. His expectation that celebrating the holiday a week earlier would generate more income for businesses did not come to fruition, leading to the holiday's return to its original day.

Ivy and Caroline planned a turkey dinner with all the trimmings to help boost everyone's spirits. The Buchanans attended, and Helen baked three pies for dessert: apple, peach, and pecan. Although the thought of war loomed in the back of everyone's mind, there was an unspoken understanding that it wouldn't be mentioned, at least on this one day. Hank led the prayer before dinner, giving thanks for all those gathered around the table and blessings to those who were not present.

November 27, 1941

Dear Diary,

Today we celebrated another holiday in our home with friends and family. I realized how blessed we are to be surrounded by those we love. Lily enjoyed her first taste of mashed potatoes, most of which landed on her bib. The laughter we shared made the house come alive as new memories were created. Maybe next year there will be another little one at the table!

A little over one week later, their world shattered. On Sunday, December 7, 1941, the Japanese bombed Pearl Harbor in a surprise attack on the U.S. Naval Base in Hawaii. Within an hour, the battleship USS *Arizona* was completely destroyed. The other ships in the harbor were severely damaged, with numerous casualties.

Ivy listened to President Roosevelt's speech on the radio. "Yesterday, December 7, 1941—a date which will live in infamy—the United States of America was suddenly and deliberately attacked by the naval and air forces of the Empire of Japan." The United States was now at war.

Profoundly saddened by this horrific and devastating news, Ivy feared the inevitable. Hank would be called up immediately to join James and Preston. Her worst nightmare was coming true, and she panicked.

Instinctively, Ivy ran to the nursery where Lily slept. She lifted her up and held her securely in her arms. Ivy shook uncontrollably as tears began to spill onto Lily's blanket. She shuddered at the thought of Hank marching off to war and leaving their happy home and the life they had just started to build together. *Whatever will we do?*

Hank was visiting his father when he heard the news of the attack on Pearl Harbor. He, like many other men, had a limited amount of time before leaving to serve his country.

"We are at war now, son. Our lives are about to change forever."

"It appears to be true. I've got to get home to Ivy right away."

The air hung still in the house, and a sense of doom lingered. Hank called out to Ivy, but she didn't answer. He looked for her in the kitchen and the parlor. When he didn't find her in either place, he ran upstairs. Ascending the staircase two steps at a time, he rushed into the nursery where Ivy sat holding Lily. He was met with a vacant stare as Ivy appeared to be a thousand miles away. Hank rushed to her side and knelt beside the rocker.

"I take it you've heard the news," he declared, knowing she was well aware of the dire situation. He could tell by the redness and puffiness of her eyes that she had been crying for quite a while.

Ivy stared past Hank, her eyes refusing to meet his, and he feared she was in shock. He put Lily in her crib and returned to Ivy. He put his arms around her to comfort her, but her limbs went limp against him. He carried her into their room and laid her on the bed. Her skin felt as cold as ice, so he covered her with the soft wool blanket they kept at the foot of their bed.

"Please, my darling, try to get ahold of yourself."

She turned to look at him and burst into tears once again. "Hank, you can't go, you just can't," she protested. "Lily and I need you here."

"You know that you and Lily are my whole life, but the world is collapsing around us. Soon, I will be called up to join the others, including both our brothers and many of our neighbors and friends, who are doing their part for the war effort. I have to help them defend our country and our life as we know it. Once this is over, I'll come home, and we can start working on a sister or brother for Lily," Hank assured her.

He took his responsibilities very seriously, but Ivy couldn't comprehend the thought of his sacrificing his life. She felt consumed with worry; her body ached with an indescribable pain she had never experienced before.

Hank lay next to Ivy until she fell asleep from exhaustion, remaining awake by her side throughout the night. When her breathing became ragged and strained, he whispered in her ear, "I love you, Ivy. I always have and always will." His words calmed her, and she fell into a peaceful rest.

December 28, 1941

Dear Diary,

As I write these words, my darling Hank is packing to leave for basic training at Fort Jackson. I can scarcely look him in the eye without crying, but I know I must try to be brave, for his sake.

Lily has no idea that her daddy is going away. She is far too young to understand the gravity of the situation, and for that, I'm thankful. At least I have Caroline here to help me, and Ben Buchanan is close by. His history of childhood rheumatic fever kept him from being drafted. Helen, too, is a source of strength, companionship, and comfort, and I know I will rely on her friendship in the days and months ahead.

I pray my Hank will come back to me very soon and we can return to our life together. Please, Lord, watch over him and protect him, our brothers, and all the other soldiers.

The war affected everyone in some way. Even First Lady Eleanor Roosevelt knew the heartbreak of saying goodbye to her loved ones. Her four sons, James, Elliott, Franklin Jr., and John, all joined the U.S. Armed Forces and served overseas.

As the clouds hung heavily in the dark afternoon sky, Hank stood on the front porch preparing to leave. His father offered to drive him to Fort Jackson along with a few other men from the bank who were also drafted. Ivy resolved to be strong and see Hank off with the image of her smiling face as she held Lily in her arms. There would be no tears today; they would come later. Ivy put on a brave face to show Hank that she and Lily would be okay in his absence. After their final kiss goodbye, he got into the car. She waved to Hank until only a trail of dust remained on the road. Her life without her husband by her side was about to begin. Hopefully, it would only be for a short time.

Chapter Ten

Charleston, SC – 1989

LANEY TRIED TO IMAGINE the emotions her grandmother experienced as she watched her husband go off to war. The fear of losing him, the uncertainty of their future, and the prospect of raising a daughter alone must have been overwhelming for Ivy. Laney could relate to feelings of apprehension surrounding an unknown future. *Oh, Grandma, your bravery is inspiring.*

After working on the house for the past week, Laney needed to relax and unwind. She thought a drive to the waterfront on this beautiful spring day would do her a world of good. As a young girl, she shared many happy times with her grandmother at the beach, sunbathing and searching for seashells in the sand. They enjoyed going to Folly Beach, where they could see the Morris Island Lighthouse from the shoreline. Revisiting the places and memories she'd shared with her grandmother made her feel closer to Ivy.

She arrived around ten in the morning, and although the forecast called for temperatures in the upper 70s that afternoon, it was still early enough to need a light jacket. Laney's skin was quite pale after a long New York winter with little time spent in the sunshine. She donned a wide-brimmed straw hat from Ivy's closet to protect her skin from burning as she walked along the shore.

The tourists had not yet arrived for the season, allowing Laney to enjoy the solitude while soaking up the sunshine. She inhaled the salty sea air and felt the ocean mist as the waves met the shoreline. She removed her sandals and tiptoed into the cool water as it swirled around her ankles before rushing out with the tide. Tiny shells collected on the sand. She gathered a few in her hands, keeping the intact ones and discarding any that were cracked or chipped.

Reflecting on the recent events, Laney realized she was at a crossroads in her life. Being back in Charleston, surrounded by familiar places and people she loved, evoked a sense of belonging. While she enjoyed her career in the restaurant, she asked herself if living in New York was right for her. She had acquaintances in New York but didn't consider them close enough to confide in or trust with personal details of her life. In the south, people cared about their neighbors and friends. After being back home for a short time, Laney was immediately embraced by not only Chase and his family but also all of Ivy's friends who had sent their condolences.

She realized she had missed the laid-back lifestyle of Charleston compared to the hustle and bustle of the Upper East Coast. Her apartment was compact, economical, and convenient, whereas Ivy's house was a home meant for a family to create happy memories for many generations. Several diary entries mentioned that Hank and Ivy shared this vision when they bought the house in 1940. Having died so young, Laney's mother never had the chance to fulfill her parents' dream, but Ivy instilled strong family values in Laney to perpetuate the family heritage. Laney couldn't ignore the ties to her past.

There was much to consider in moving back to Charleston. She would have to leave her job; however, with her inheritance, there was no sense of urgency to find another one. She could leave what little furniture she had at the apartment since many renters in the city were looking for furnished places. Although dated and old-fashioned, Laney could remodel Ivy's house by replacing or adding pieces as she liked. Her mind began reeling with excitement. The more she thought about it, the better it sounded. *Goodbye, New York, I'm going home!*

Realizing she was at least two miles from where she started walking, Laney quickly turned around and walked back to her car, thinking of details the entire way. She wondered what Chase would think of the idea. Last night, they had been closer than ever before, and it felt so right. She couldn't wait to share the news with him.

She called Chase but got his answering machine, so she called his parents' house. Mrs. Buchanan heard the phone ringing in the kitchen and ran to answer it.

"Hello?"

"Hi, Mrs. B, this is Laney. I was wondering if Chase is there."

"Hi, Laney. No, Chase isn't here right now. He and his dad went into Charleston to look at farm equipment. They should be back soon. I can have him call you when he gets back."

"Thanks, that would be great."

"Laney, I wanted to ask you about the memorial service for Ivy. I know all of Ivy's friends and can help with the preparations. We can have it here at our house."

"I would appreciate your help, Mrs. B."

The two met that afternoon to work out the details. The service would be held the following Sunday at one in the afternoon. The guest list was small enough to reach everyone by phone, and Mrs. Buchanan would make all the calls. Laney would prepare a light luncheon of sandwiches, salads, and punch. Mrs. Buchanan's desserts would round out the meal, including her famous Ambrosia salad.

As they finalized their plans, Mrs. Buchanan's curiosity got the best of her, and she broached the subject of Ivy's house with Laney.

"Have you given any thought to what you'll do now that you have inherited your grandmother's house?"

Laney knew the question would eventually come up. She wanted to wait to let Chase be the first to hear of her decision about moving back to Charleston, but she couldn't contain her excitement any longer.

"Actually, I've given it a lot of thought."

Mrs. Buchanan hoped that Laney would move back to Charleston. Ever since Laney and Chase were children, she had dreamed that one day they would get together. They were compatible on so many levels and seemed perfect for each other. When they went in opposite directions after high school, she gave up hope of them becoming a couple, but things had now changed, and she became optimistic once again.

Laney and Mrs. Buchanan had always been close, especially when she was an adolescent trying to find her way. It was Chase's mom who found Laney crying one day, thinking she was going to die. She explained to Laney that she wasn't dying, just becoming a woman. She bought Laney her first package of feminine products and a new pair of blue jeans. Not having a daughter of her own, Mrs. Buchanan welcomed the occasions when Laney needed mothering and never hesitated to help nurture her. Of course, she had Ivy, but the relationship with a grandmother is different, and Laney felt more at ease talking about certain things with Chase's mom.

"I've decided to come back home to Charleston and live in my grandmother's house."

Unable to hide her feelings, Mrs. Buchanan leaped from her chair and hugged Laney. "I hoped you would say that!" she exclaimed.

Laney returned her warm embrace, and they stood hugging for a long while. "I haven't had a chance to tell Chase yet."

"I'm sure he'll be thrilled. Don't worry, I won't spill the beans," she assured Laney.

"Do you really think he'll be happy about me moving back?"

"Of course! You and Chase have always been like two peas in a pod."

Her words encouraged Laney. They hugged again and were both crying happy tears as Chase's dad walked through the door.

"What's going on in here?" Mr. Buchanan asked.

"Nothing, Joe, just girl talk," Mrs. B. shrugged with a grin and a wink toward Laney.

Satisfied with her explanation, he didn't press the issue. "Okay. Chase is outside with the new baler we picked up in town. I'll tell him to come in to say hello." He grabbed two apples from the fruit bowl on the table and went back outside to the barn.

"Where've you been, Dad?"

Joe tossed an apple to Chase. "Talking to your mom and Laney. They're inside planning Ivy's memorial service."

"Speaking of Laney, I wanted to ask you if you remember anything about her parents."

"Why do you ask, son?"

Respecting her privacy, Chase didn't reveal the full details of Ivy's letter to Laney, only that there were some questions about what happened to her mother and father.

"Laney wants to learn more about her family and asked if I had any information I could share with her."

"Lily Spencer and I were close in age and went to school together, but she ran with a different crowd. I recall her as somewhat of a rebel, always getting into things she shouldn't have; particularly when it came to boys."

"Couldn't Ivy stop her?"

"Lord knows she tried. Once, while I was delivering hay bales to Ivy, I overheard Lily and Ivy fighting about where she was going and with whom. Their heated row ended in Lily storming out of the house and taking off with friends Ivy didn't like."

"Is that how she met Laney's father?"

"Yes. I didn't know Peter well, but I knew that he came from the wrong side of the tracks. Trouble seemed to follow him wherever he went, and he never amounted to anything or held down a job. I was surprised to hear they got married."

"Were you here when they died?"

"Yes. I remember hearing the awful news about the car crash," Joe said as he described the events with sadness. "Ivy was devastated, and our family stayed close to her during those dark days. The newspaper didn't report much about the accident, saying only that they both perished in the fire."

"Do you know anything about Preston Spencer?"

"No, he was closer in age to my Uncle Billy, your Grandpa Ben's brother. I believe they served in the war together."

Chase could tell that his dad didn't have much information, so he dropped it and changed the subject. "It sure is nice seeing Laney again."

"You two used to be so close growing up. Why did you lose touch?"

"After high school, we went our separate ways and got busy. She carved out a career for herself in New York."

"She's quite an accomplished young lady. Ever think about starting a relationship with her? You've never dated much after you and Charlene called it quits."

"That was years ago, and never anything serious. She wasn't the right one for me, and to be honest, I haven't had time for a relationship. I've thought about Laney from time to time, but there was too much distance between us to get together. Not saying I didn't want to."

"No time like the present, son. Why don't you poke your head in and say hello?"

Chase walked back to the house as his mother came outside, heading to her car. "Where are you off to?"

"I have a few errands to run," she told him, smiling coyly.

"Okay, see you later, Mom."

Laney was sitting at the kitchen table when Chase walked in the back door. "Hey there. What's up, Lane?"

"Your mom and I were finalizing the arrangements for the memorial service next Sunday."

"Let me know what I can do to help. I can set up chairs and tables or anything else you need me to do."

Laney thanked him. She started telling him she wanted to talk to him about something, and at the same time, Chase told her he had something to tell her. They both laughed and waited for the other to start.

"You go first, Chase."

He told Laney that he'd asked his dad about her father and Preston Spencer. Laney paid close attention, hoping he had new information.

"Dad said he didn't know much about what happened or about your great uncle, but told me that my great uncle Billy and Preston were buddies."

"Really? Is he still alive?"

"Yes. He lives in a nursing home the next town over. I can try to arrange a visit with him."

Given his advanced age, Laney tried not to get overly optimistic about the possibility that his uncle would remember much from so many years ago. "Thanks, Chase. I appreciate that. Maybe we can visit him when things settle down a bit."

"I think that's best, at least for a while. You have a lot going on with the memorial service and getting ready to go back to New York next week."

"That's what I wanted to talk to you about. I've thought it through, and I've decided to return to Charleston and move back into my grandmother's house."

"Are you sure? That's a big step. What about your job at the restaurant, and your apartment?"

She had hoped he'd be thrilled at the thought of her being right next door again, but his matter-of-fact tone held little emotion. *Does he think it isn't a good idea? Did I misinterpret his signs of affection? Was he just being neighborly by offering to help me?*

She had to know his thoughts about not only her plans to move back, but what the future might hold for the two of them.

"New York City isn't the right place for me. Career-wise, it's a good choice, but after living there these past few years, I realize I'm not a city girl. Being here has shown me how much I've missed living in a home, rather than an apartment, and breathing fresh air and listening to the wind blow through the trees, not the sounds of sirens and traffic."

"Those are all great reasons. With your talent, there's no telling how far you can go in Charleston—maybe own your own place."

Laney felt a little relieved after hearing that Chase understood her decision, but still wanted to know about his feelings toward her. "I also realized how much I've missed you." *There, it was out in the open now.* She waited for his response.

"Same here, Laney."

She decided to leave it at that, remembering that Chase could be a closed book at times. "I'd better get back home. I have to make several calls to set these plans in motion."

Chase sensed Laney's disappointment from his subtle reaction to her news. He was indeed happy to learn she would be coming back to Charleston, but had a difficult time sharing his feelings. Laney got up to leave, but Chase stopped her.

"Laney, please don't get me wrong. I think it's great that you're moving back."

He closed the gap between them and bent his head toward hers. She lifted her gaze to meet his, and he gently kissed her lips. As his arms encircled her, their kiss deepened. They parted briefly, stared into each other's eyes, then kissed again.

Chase paused and said, "I didn't plan on that happening."

"I'm not sorry it did, Chase, are you?" Laney leaned into him with a soft sigh.

"No, I reckon it's about time," he told her with a playful smile.

At that moment, everything changed. What started as a childhood friendship began to evolve into an adult romance. It was exhilarating and scary at the same time. Laney wasn't certain where they were headed, but she knew it felt right.

"Call me later, Chase," she requested. He gave her a quick kiss on the forehead and promised to call her after helping his dad with the new equipment.

Laney went home and called the restaurant to tell her boss that she would be leaving. Disappointed, he tried to talk her into changing her mind. Laney stuck to her decision and thanked him for all he had done for her.

Next, she called her landlord to tell him she would be leaving at the end of the month. Since Laney had lived there for several years and had a month-to-month lease, she didn't have to worry about subletting the apartment. Her landlord assured her it wouldn't be difficult to rent it and asked her permission to show it to prospective tenants.

"Of course you can," Laney told him. "I'll be back next week to move my things out and get it cleaned up."

Suddenly, Ivy's house felt different to Laney. She would officially be moving back home as mistress of the house. She had never owned a home before. There were many things she needed to learn about, like insurance, taxes, and hot water heaters. Her grandmother was always on top of things, and Laney would begin reviewing her records after returning from New York.

For now, she would start changing her address back to 5037 Cypress Lane. Seeing it written on paper made Laney excited, and she felt deep down that she'd made the right decision. Coupled with the new direction in her relationship with Chase, it seemed all the more sound.

After eating a light dinner, Laney decided to relax for a while until Chase called. She picked up reading where she left off in Ivy's diary. Laney couldn't help but feel that she and her grandmother, with her husband leaving to fight in World War II, faced similar situations by needing to learn how to run this big house alone. She hoped she would glean valuable information from Ivy's diary to help her navigate these uncharted waters.

Chapter Eleven

Charleston, SC – 1942

IVY PULLED HERSELF UP by her bootstraps and reevaluated her life with Hank away at war. Mrs. Roosevelt said, "With the new day comes new strength and new thoughts." She needed new thoughts about taking care of Lily, the household chores, and whatever else came her way.

Before leaving, Hank left detailed instructions on paying the bills and managing their checking account. He also provided a list of important people to contact if Ivy needed anything, including the name of his lawyer and accountant. He taught Ivy how to drive their car so she would have a means of getting around. Her parents were close by, which made her feel a little better about being alone.

Hank's first letter arrived in the mail. His basic training in Fort Jackson would be completed by the end of the month, and he'd be home on leave for one week before shipping out. He wasn't certain yet where he would be stationed and couldn't tell her even if he knew.

Ivy spotted Hank in the crowd of soldiers at the bus station and ran into his arms. Seeing him in his uniform with his hair cropped short for the first time, she remarked, "You look so handsome!"

Hank took a step back to study her. "You're a sight for sore eyes."

Walking back to the car arm in arm, Hank asked, "How's your driving coming along?"

"I'm getting better at it, but still need a little more practice. Do you want to drive home, or shall I?"

"I'm exhausted from the long bus ride. Would you mind driving?"

Ivy got behind the wheel and drove back to Cypress Lane. Caroline had just given Lily her bath when Hank came running upstairs. He scooped her up and inhaled the sweet scent of his daughter, playfully tickling her. She giggled with delight and snuggled into his chest.

Ivy tried her best to make Hank's week home enjoyable, purposely avoiding the subject of the war. They strolled around the pond with Lily, dined with their families, and enjoyed quiet times together. She cooked Hank's favorite dishes and desserts, knowing he wouldn't be fed well in the service. Each night, they made love with a heightened sense of passion and desire. Ivy missed the feel of Hank's touch on her body and made a mental imprint of each sensation.

Hank's appetite was voracious. Ivy made him a big breakfast complete with eggs, hash browns, biscuits, and gravy.

"You could teach the Army a few things about cooking."

"I've come a long way, and Caroline has taught me a thing or two."

"Not only the cooking, Ivy. You've done a great job keeping the house running smoothly. I'm so proud of you."

"I tried my best, Hank."

When the time came for Hank to leave, Ivy once again put on a brave face. As they embraced at the bus station one last time, Ivy took her monogrammed lace handkerchief out of her purse and slipped it into Hank's hand.

"Carry this with you. Let it be a reminder that I'm with you in thought until we're reunited."

Hank choked up as he placed the handkerchief in his breast pocket. "I will keep it next to my heart, just as I do you," he told her.

Hank heard his company being called to board the bus and ran to join the other soldiers. Pausing at the door, he turned back for one last look at Ivy. She watched as he walked down the narrow aisle and took a seat. He waved goodbye to her through the window as the bus pulled away. Just that quickly, he was gone. Ivy stood frozen for a long time, feeling as if she were being torn in two. She gathered herself together and went home.

April 8, 1942

Dear Diary,

The waiting begins, for letters from Hank with word that he is safe and for the day when he returns home to Lily and me. I must find ways to keep occupied or else the anticipation will drive me to madness. There are many things I can do at home to support the war effort. If Hank can make sacrifices, then so shall I.

Charleston, SC – 1989

Laney shuddered as she read about how the war had changed Ivy's life. She must have been terrified to be alone, but still found ways to cope. Laney hoped to channel Ivy's resilience amid all the changes in her own life. When Chase called later that night, Laney told him she was in awe of Ivy's bravery.

"You come from good stock, and I'm sure you inherited all the good qualities Ivy possessed."

"She inspires me and gives me the courage to face whatever my future holds."

The morning of the memorial service, the Buchanans were busy setting up and preparing for the guests to arrive. Buddy parked himself under a shady Magnolia tree for the afternoon to avoid the commotion. The pastor from Ivy's church delivered a touching eulogy praising Ivy for her generosity, graciousness, and genuine concern for her friends and neighbors. Guests were invited to say a few words about Ivy.

"Ivy was a pillar in our community, always giving to those in need," remarked a neighbor. Similar stories from friends about how Ivy had touched each one of their lives endeared her to Laney all the more.

A woman who Laney didn't recognize began to speak, and she was anxious to hear her remarks.

"My name is Deidre, and I'm the daughter of Caroline, Lily's nanny."

Laney was intrigued to discover her identity and listened intently to everything she shared.

"Lily and I were childhood companions, and I enjoyed many happy times at Ivy's home. During the war, Ivy and my mother supported each other while both their husbands were overseas. Ivy's generosity and love helped us all through a very difficult time, and I'm eternally grateful for all she did for my family."

Deidre returned to her seat. Afterward, Laney sought her out, eager to ask questions about her mother. She hoped she had insight about what had happened to Lily and Peter.

Laney introduced herself. "Hello, Deidre, I'm Laney Armstrong, Lily's daughter."

"Hello, Laney. I'm so sorry for the loss of your grandmother."

"Thank you," Laney replied, "and thank you for your kind words about her."

The two chatted for a while, and Laney asked if they could get together at a later date to talk more about Ivy, Caroline, and Lily.

"Of course. I have fond memories of growing up with Ivy and your mother. We drifted apart in high school, after she..." Deidre stopped herself from finishing the sentence. She hadn't thought about the falling-out with Lily in a long time and felt uncomfortable discussing it.

Laney wondered what Deidre was referring to, but this wasn't the time or place to delve into the events of the past.

"I'm leaving for New York to close my apartment out, but I'll call you when I return to Charleston." They exchanged phone numbers and planned to meet again soon. Deidre said her goodbyes and left the gathering.

"Looks like you made a new friend," Chase remarked as he sat down next to her.

"Yes! Her mother was my mother's nanny, and they grew up together. I hope she might have some details surrounding her death. We're getting together after I return from New York."

"When are you leaving?"

"I plan on heading out early tomorrow morning."

"Have you thought about how you're going to get all your stuff back home?"

"I don't have much since my apartment is pretty small, and I'm leaving all the furniture behind. I thought I might fit everything in my car."

"I doubt your Mustang will hold very much. If you like, I can drive up with you, and we can put everything in the back of the truck."

"Are you sure your dad can manage without you for a few days?"

"Of course. Besides, I'm sure you don't want to make that long trip alone again."

"Thanks, Chase. That would be a big help," she admitted. "I'd love the company and help with packing and moving."

"It's been an emotional day, Lane. You should go home and get to bed early. I'll swing by and pick you up at seven, okay?"

Laney agreed. The memorial service had drained her, and she looked forward to some much-needed rest. He kissed her goodbye as if it were the most natural thing to do. Laney smiled at him and felt like they were becoming a couple. After such a long day, the small moment felt like a promise of something good ahead.

Chapter Twelve

Charleston, SC – 1989

L ANEY GOT UP AT six, dressed in jeans and an oversized sweatshirt, ate breakfast, and waited for Chase. The rising sun in the cloudless sky held the promise of a perfect spring day. March was going out like a lamb, with temperatures in the mid-sixties. The dogwoods and forsythia were in full bloom. The eastern redbuds were showing off their spectacular purple-pink flowers, adding to the colorful show of spring. With a little luck, they'd see the cherry blossom trees while driving through Washington, DC.

In preparation for the trip, Laney gathered cleaning supplies and snacks for the road. Most of her clothes and toiletries were still back in New York, so she didn't need to pack personal items. She hoped to make the drive in one day, spend one day packing, and return the following day so Chase wouldn't be gone too long. It suddenly occurred to her that they would have to spend two nights alone together. *How is this going to work? There's only one bedroom in the apartment, and the apartment-size sofa is too small and uncomfortable for Chase to sleep on.*

She wondered if Chase factored in being away together for a couple of nights when he offered to help her move. Certainly, they weren't at the point where they would sleep together. Laney wasn't ready to move that fast. Before she could give it more thought, Chase pulled into the driveway. *Oh well, we'll just have to wait and see what happens.*

Buddy jumped out of the back of Chase's truck and ran up the front steps to meet Laney at the door. Frisky as usual, he waited to be petted.

"Good morning, Buddy boy," she said, briskly rubbing her hands through the thick fur on his neck. "Are you coming to New York too?"

"If he had his way, he'd be in the front seat, but no, he isn't coming."

"Too bad. I'm really growing quite fond of him. It's nice to have a dog around the house."

Chase noticed the affection Laney showed Buddy and made a mental note to himself.

"Are you all set to go?"

"Yes. I just have a few things to take with us. Let me grab them and lock up."

"Okay. My dad will keep an eye on the house while we're gone."

They loaded the cleaning supplies in the back and put the small cooler behind the seat of the truck. Chase yelled at Buddy to go back home, and they set out on the long road trip ahead of them. Chase estimated they would make it to New York by seven that night with a few short stops along the way.

Laney decided not to worry about the sleeping arrangements. Instead, she kept the conversation light and easygoing. Laney talked about her ambitions of starting a small restaurant one day. Chase told her of his desire to keep the Buchanan family farming tradition going strong for many years to come.

"I admire your dedication to family and strong work ethic, Chase. Tradition is important to both of us, isn't it?"

"I wouldn't have it any other way," Chase agreed.

"It's rare to find someone who understands that. Most of the people I've met in New York are only concerned about how far they can go, no matter what the cost. They're not the type of people I wanted to associate with."

"Perhaps, but I bet there were a lot of guys beating down your door."

"No, not at all," Laney said, surprised that Chase would think that to be the case. "I worked so many late nights at the restaurant, I barely had time for myself, let alone a relationship.

"What about you, Chase? Have you dated much these past few years?"

"Same as you, Lane...no time."

"No one?"

"Maybe one girl for a short while, but it didn't work out. She hated farm life and country living. We were worlds apart in what we wanted."

"I can understand that. Not everyone appreciates the peacefulness of a summer night under the stars listening to the katydids."

"You do! That's why you stole my heart the first day I met you, and I've been smitten ever since," Chase said with a grin.

Laney studied his expression, unsure whether he was serious or teasing.

New York City, NY – 1989

They arrived in New York a little after rush hour and went straight to Laney's apartment. They were both famished and exhausted from the long drive, so she ordered Chinese food and had it delivered. After dinner, it was too late to start packing, so they just relaxed for the rest of the night.

"I like your apartment, Laney. It's cozy."

"Thanks. It's been a great first apartment, but I'm happy to go back to living in a real home."

"I can't argue with that, Lane," said Chase, letting out a long yawn. "I'm beat, how 'bout you?"

"Yes, me too."

Chase looked around the apartment and realized there wasn't a place for him to sleep. He noticed Laney nervously biting her lower lip.

"I'll just run down to my truck and grab my sleeping bag and camp out here on the living room floor."

"Are you sure, Chase? You can have the bed, and I'll sleep on the sofa."

"I'll be fine right here. It'll be like when we used to camp outside in the summertime."

Laney smiled at the mention of their shared memory. She went to get a pillow for Chase while he unrolled his sleeping bag on the floor.

Laney used the bathroom first and crossed the living room on her way to the bedroom, wearing her nightshirt. Chase took note of her slender figure silhouetted beneath the thin fabric. He walked toward the bathroom and caught her scent lingering in the air. *Was she wearing that perfume before? How have I not noticed that beautiful body?* He tried to brush these thoughts out of his mind, but couldn't.

"Good night, Chase, sweet dreams."

"Uh, you too, Lane," he stammered. *Was she kidding*? The sight of Laney would be the only thing he'd be dreaming about that night.

Chase's thoughts kept him awake most of the night. He wondered if his casual comment about stealing his heart reflected his true feelings. He and Laney were friends for so long that he never saw her as a girlfriend. But why not? Laney was everything he desired in a woman. Strong and independent with a good head for business, she worked hard to attain her dreams. *I must be an idiot. She's been right in front of me my entire life, but I feel like I'm just seeing her for the first time.*

Chase finally fell asleep just as the rising sun steadily crept through the kitchen window.

Only a couple of hours later, Laney rose and got dressed. She made a pot of strong coffee, knowing it would be a long and busy day. In addition to packing, she needed to cancel her utility and telephone accounts, close her bank account, and give her forwarding address to the post office. Later on, she'd stop by the restaurant to say goodbye and pick up her final paycheck.

Chase started to stir inside his sleeping bag. He rolled over and saw Laney sitting at the kitchen table.

"Have you been up long?"

"No, just long enough to make coffee and plan the day. I thought we'd have a good breakfast before getting started."

"Sounds good to me."

They ate breakfast, cleaned up the kitchen, and started packing. Her landlord had conveniently put some boxes in the hallway for her to use. They worked together for about two hours and made substantial progress. Chase packed boxes and stacked them in the corner of the living room while Laney cleaned out cabinets and closets, scrubbed the bathroom, and emptied out the refrigerator. The close quarters of the small apartment made it challenging to stay out of each other's way. Remembering how Laney looked last night, Chase could barely contain himself each time they collided.

Laney washed her hands in the kitchen sink and spun around to grab the towel when she ran right into Chase's chest. Instinctively, he wrapped his arms around her and pulled her close to him. He bent down to kiss her, and she welcomed his eager lips. She, too, felt the tension in the air each time Chase was near her. She wrapped her arms around his neck, and their kiss deepened, unleashing a fervid passion inside her. Breathless, they paused for a moment.

Chase pressed his body against hers. He slid his hands up and down her back, caressing her. His touch sent a quiet shiver through her body.

"Oh, Chase."

"Laney," he murmured back, as he began kissing her again, this time more slowly and deliberately, savoring the taste of her.

A loud knock at the door jolted them out of their embrace.

"Miss Armstrong," her landlord yelled through the closed door, "are you home?"

Laney hastily composed herself. "Yes, I'm here," she yelled back as she crossed the apartment to open the door.

"I'm sorry to bother you, but I wondered if I could show your apartment this afternoon."

"Yes, of course," Laney told him, still recovering from the passionate encounter with Chase.

"Okay, I'll be by around three."

"That's fine, and thanks for the boxes."

Laney closed the door and went to find Chase, who was sweating heavily from carrying heavy boxes from the bedroom into the living room.

"What's in these boxes, Lane? They weigh a ton."

"Cookbooks, of course," she said matter-of-factly. "I just spoke to my landlord; he's showing the apartment at three, so we need to be out at that time."

"Okay. We can get your check, pick up dinner and start loading the truck after we eat. I think we can get it done tonight and leave for home first thing in the morning."

"Good plan."

Working side by side for the rest of the day, they got everything packed and cleaned. At the restaurant, Laney introduced Chase to her boss, who insisted on treating them both to dinner. "This is one amazing lady, Mr. Buchanan. You're a lucky man."

"I think so too," Chase told him, all the while smiling at Laney.

By the time they loaded the last box on the truck, they were both exhausted. Laney's landlord let them park it inside his garage for safekeeping overnight.

"I must have climbed those stairs at least fifty times today," said Chase, yawning and stretching his arms.

"You look so tired."

"I'll be okay after a little shut-eye."

Laney felt bad about Chase sleeping another night on the floor in that uncomfortable sleeping bag. She didn't want to seem forward but didn't want him to suffer. *They could sleep together in the bed without any expectations. Couldn't they?*

"Chase, please sleep in the bed tonight."

"Laney, I can't do that. Besides, where would you sleep?"

When Laney didn't answer, he realized she meant they would both share the bed.

"Are you sure, Lane?"

"Yes, I'm sure," she told him. Compelled to clarify her offer, she added, "Please don't misunderstand me. It's just for tonight... It's the logical thing to do."

Apprehensively, he agreed, and they both got ready for bed.

Laney slipped into bed while Chase was brushing his teeth. She hoped her nervousness wasn't too evident. He got into bed alongside her. Neither of them said a word or moved for a moment. Finally, Chase cleared his throat.

"I bet you're glad we got the place packed up. Tomorrow you'll be on your way to starting your new life in Charleston."

"Yes. I'm more than ready for this change."

There were so many questions she wanted to ask him, such as: Where is their relationship headed? Thankfully, the darkness of the room hid her awkwardness, making it easier to talk without looking at him directly.

"Chase," she began, "I hope you'll be a part of my new life. I mean, I want us to be, well...you know." She didn't quite know how to say what she wanted to. "It's just that..." she started again, then hesitated.

Chase felt just as uneasy and tried to help her. "I think I know what you're trying to say, Laney."

But did he really? Laney wasn't sure if he was thinking along the same lines as her.

"Laney, it's been a little strange these past couple of weeks. Things between us have changed a lot since the last time we saw each other."

"Is that good or bad, Chase?"

"It's good, but I wasn't expecting it," he answered, trying desperately not to hurt her feelings. "Just takes a little getting used to," he added.

"I hadn't expected it either, Chase."

Laney got very quiet, and Chase thought he had said the wrong thing. He turned on his side to face her, and she did the same. Even through the darkness, he could see the outline of her face, the contour of her cheeks, and the fullness of her lips. He spoke with a warm tenderness in his voice.

"This trip made me realize something, Lane."

"And what is it you realized?" she asked, holding her breath for his response.

"That I'm in love with you and have been all my life."

Those were the words she'd hoped to hear. *He loves me and always has!* She knew it was a big step for Chase to convey his feelings toward her.

"Oh, Chase, I love you too. From the first time you tickled my foot in the meadow."

He wrapped his arms around her and held her with a fierce intensity. Laney never felt as wanted and secure as she did at that moment. She had never really shaken feelings of loneliness after the loss of her parents. Ivy had done her best to fill that void, but when Ivy died, Laney's sense of emptiness returned. Reconnecting with Chase made Laney realize how deeply she yearned to love and be loved.

Laney closed her eyes and nestled into Chase's body. Exhausted, they both drifted off to sleep, the rise and fall of their chests matching perfectly. It was the beginning of many new and exciting changes for them.

Early the next morning, Laney and Chase were on their way back home. The drive gave them a chance not only to get reacquainted but to talk about what might be on the horizon.

"Tell me the truth... Will you miss New York City?"

"There are certain things I'll miss, like my job and seeing Broadway shows regularly, but that's about it."

"I guess I'm just a farm boy at heart. New York is not my cup of tea."

Laney chuckled at his proclamation and pictured him as a scruffy little boy in bib overalls with a piece of straw dangling from his mouth. He still had that boyish charm that first attracted her to him.

"What will you do first when you get back home, Lane?"

Her heart melted whenever he called her Lane. Only Chase called her that, and she loved that he had a pet name for her.

"I want to meet with Deidre and see if she can tell me more about my mother. There are so many secrets and mysteries surrounding her death. I hope that by talking to people who knew her, I can find out more about the night she died and maybe learn what happened to my father."

Chase found himself being protective of Laney, not wanting her to be hurt in any way. "Are you sure you want to uncover things that happened so long ago?"

"Yes, I'm sure, Chase. My grandmother carried regret and guilt for most of her life. I feel like if I can find out the truth, it would somehow exonerate her and set her free, at least in my eyes."

Chase understood and promised to help in any way he could. "Together, we'll do whatever we can to make that happen," he said as he reached over and squeezed her hand.

"Thanks, Chase," she said, her eyes smiling at him.

Shortly after seven o'clock that evening, Chase pulled his truck into Laney's driveway. She suggested he drop her off and come back tomorrow to unload the boxes from the truck. Chase agreed. He walked Laney up to the front door and followed her inside.

"Get some rest. I'll be by sometime in the morning to help you with the boxes." Resisting the temptation to linger, Chase kissed her goodnight and went home.

Chapter Thirteen

Charleston, SC – 1989

I T WAS NEARLY LUNCHTIME, and Laney hadn't seen Chase yet. She made herself a sandwich and started eating when she heard a familiar scratching at the back door. She had wondered how long it would take Buddy to drop by to welcome her back home.

"Okay, Buddy, I'm coming," she called out. But to her surprise, when Laney opened the door, it wasn't Buddy standing on the back porch but a miniature version of him. Surprised to see a chipper little puppy, Laney bent down and scooped him up into her arms.

"Who are you?" she asked as the puppy squirmed in her hands and licked her face. Laney fell to the floor laughing and played with the spunky little bundle of energy. He started running circles around her.

"My goodness," Laney exclaimed, "what a little rascal you are!"

Chase appeared in the doorway, laughing along with Laney. "I think you just named your new puppy. Laney, meet Rascal."

"What do you mean? Is this my dog?"

"Yes, unless you don't want him," said Chase as he joined Laney on the floor to play with the puppy.

"Of course I do! Where did you get him?"

"From the same breeder where I got Buddy. They had a new litter of puppies about two months ago, and I called this morning to see if there were any left. Sure enough, this little fellow hadn't been claimed, so I ran over and got him."

Buddy came bolting through the back door, and the two dogs took an instant liking to each other. They ran outside to play in the yard as Laney and Chase stood at the door watching them roll and frolic together.

Chase slipped his arm around Laney and said, "Those two will get along great."

"One happy little family."

Chase held her close and smiled.

They unloaded the boxes from Chase's truck and Laney started unpacking while Chase went to the store for groceries and dog food. He reappeared about an hour later with not only the puppy food, but a bag full of toys and treats.

"Spoiling Rascal already, are you?"

"You'll thank me later, Lane, when he chews on these instead of the legs of the furniture!" Chase grinned, wagging a chew toy in the air.

"I guess there's a lot I need to learn about raising a puppy. By the way, I got a call this morning from Deidre. She wants to meet for lunch next Friday."

"Do you want me to come along for moral support?"

"Thank you, but I think I'll be okay."

"What kinds of questions are you planning to ask her?"

"I'm not sure yet. I'm going to read some more of Ivy's diary this week. It might give me clues about my mother's teenage years when they were friends."

"Okay, but please be careful, Lane. Some things from the past might not be worth digging up. I'll be here if you need me."

"Thanks. I appreciate your support."

That night, Laney fashioned a bed for Rascal using an old blanket. He was worn out playing with Buddy and went right to sleep. She began reading diary passages from early April 1942. Tucked between the pages was a folded letter, its edges worn with time.

Charleston, SC – 1942

"What has you so preoccupied this morning, Ivy?"

"Oh, Caroline, please excuse me for not hearing you. I received a letter from Hank this morning."

Caroline knew that letters from overseas were few and far between. She hadn't heard from her husband in several weeks and waited with bated breath for news about his safety.

"I understand. I'll leave you to it."

"Thank you, Caroline. I hope you hear from Walter soon."

Ivy read the first letter she had received since Hank shipped out.

April 3, 1942

My Dear Ivy,

I'm overseas now, somewhere in the Pacific. Censors read all letters from GIs, so I'm not at liberty to expound. Please know I'm safe and doing well. It is warm here, much like Charleston. I hope you and Lily are getting along fine. You are both in my thoughts day and night. I keep the handkerchief you gave me next to my heart at all times to keep me safe and protected. Take good care of yourself and Lily. I'll be seeing you very soon.

Your loving husband,

Hank

Ivy carefully placed the letter in her dresser drawer and continued to add each subsequent letter to the stack as they arrived. Someday, they would read them together with Lily so she would know that her daddy did his part by serving his country.

Ivy also received a letter from her brother, Preston. He hinted about his involvement with Lieutenant Colonel James Doolittle and his squadron of B-25 bombers that led the raid over Tokyo.

April 12, 1942

Dear Sis,

Please know that I'm safe and hope Hank is as well. While I can't give you specifics, I participated in a raid you may have read about. My views of the world have changed, and I fear I'm not the same man you've always known. I've seen the inhumanity of one man against another and cannot tolerate aggression and oppression without wanting to make things right. By the way, Billy Buchanan and I are in the same platoon. Please let his family know he is safe. Looking forward to coming stateside soon.

Your brother,
Preston

The morale of the country improved as Americans hailed President Roosevelt's bold attack on Japan. Telegrams barraged the White House in support of his tactical move with hopes of bringing an end to the war. On June 4, 1942, the Battle of Midway proved successful with the United States catching the Japanese by surprise. The battle continued for several days as the U.S. troops attacked at sea and on Midway, forcing the Japanese to retreat. Their navy was decimated, and they suffered staggering casualties and losses to their fleet.

July 14, 1942

My Dear Ivy,

Each day I trudge on, resolute in my faith that our President will lead us to victory. The work is hard, but our troops are strong and determined to defeat our enemies.

I'm using V-Mail to write to you. It is shorter, but the fastest way to correspond. Please write whenever you can. My heart leaps when I hear my name at Mail Call, as I look forward to news from home. Nighttime is the worst because that's when I think of you the most. I miss being there with you and Lily. I miss dancing with you in my arms and holding you close. Be strong, my dear, and soon we will be together again.

Your loving husband,

Hank

That summer, the War Production Board mandated rationing to ensure the servicemen had a sufficient supply of uniforms. Cotton and wool were needed for coats, trousers, and shirts. Ration books were distributed for purchasing food and other goods. Buyers used stamps to purchase rationed items such as sugar, flour, coffee, and cooking oil, and retailers used them to replenish their stock. Butter and sugar became scarce, and margarine and corn syrup took their place.

Victory gardens popped up all over the country to help housewives conserve their stamps for items they couldn't grow or make themselves. Ivy and Caroline planted potatoes, tomatoes, cucumbers, peas, and green beans in their little garden behind the house.

"Well, Caroline, we should be proud of ourselves; it looks like we're farmers now," quipped Ivy as she perused the garden they had planted.

"I believe so! This war has taught me many things I never dreamed I could do."

"It's the least we can do while our men are fighting to protect us."

"Amen to that, Ivy."

Rubber was in short supply as the demand to make tires for tanks and military vehicles increased. Shoes and boots were rationed, and civilians were encouraged to keep their car tires in good repair to make them last longer. The recommended speed limit became thirty-five miles per hour with slow and steady stops and turns to reduce the wear on tire treads.

In November, Macy's canceled the annual Thanksgiving Day Parade because the balloons were made of rubber and used helium to be inflated. Macy's donated all the balloons in support of the war effort. Rubber drives were held to collect surplus items such as raincoats, old boots, hot water bottles, and even the rubber pants used to cover babies' cloth diapers.

Ivy made good on her personal promise to do her part as a civilian by organizing a rubber drive. She offered her barn to store all the collected items and spread the word at her church and local establishments.

"Hello, Miss Ivy. What brings you by on this hot summer day?" asked her neighbor Ben Buchanan.

"Hi, Ben. I need your help. So many of our friends and neighbors have donated to my rubber drive. I need the use of a truck to haul the cache to the local repository."

"Have you collected a lot of things so far?"

"Yes! The response has been overwhelmingly fruitful. One lady brought her husband's favorite pair of old, worn-out boots, confiding that she was grateful for the chance to get them out of her house while he was gone!"

"I'd be happy to help. You tell me when and I'll be there."

The outcome of the drive pleased Ivy, and she wrote a letter to Hank telling him all about it. She hoped it would bolster his spirits to know she wasn't sitting home feeling sorry for herself but helping him and the rest of the soldiers in any way she could.

By the time Lily had her second birthday in March of 1943, Hank had been gone for over a year. He missed many of the precocious little things toddlers do. He sent several letters, and each one brought Ivy a sense of relief that he was still safe.

As the war raged on, the news was promising one day, distressing the next, but mostly depressing. One afternoon, while Ivy was weeding the garden, Caroline appeared at the gate with a look of horror on her face.

"Caroline, what is it? You look as if you've seen a ghost."

Barely able to utter the words, she said, "There's a man at the front door."

Ivy couldn't understand why Caroline was so upset. "It's probably someone who is lost," she said as she wiped the dirt from her hands on her apron.

"No, Ivy," replied Caroline, breaking out in a cold sweat. "He's not lost."

Ivy became increasingly concerned about Caroline's behavior. "Who is it, Caroline? Tell me!" she demanded.

"It's Western Union," she said flatly.

The two women clung to each other, knowing full well that a hand-delivered message from Western Union could only bring bad news. Not knowing for whom the telegram was intended, they both braced for the worst. Bolstering every ounce of courage she possessed, Ivy told Caroline, "We will answer the door together."

Holding on to each other for support, they walked hand in hand to the front porch to meet the deliveryman. He stepped forward, visibly upset by the paper he held in his hand. When he began to speak, both Ivy and Caroline held their breath. The man looked up at both of them to determine to whom he should give the telegram.

"Mrs. Westfield?"

Ivy's legs gave out from under her, and Caroline led her to one of the wicker chairs on the porch. Reluctantly, the deliveryman handed Ivy the distinctive yellow envelope. Ivy reached out her trembling hand and took the telegram, saying nothing. Caroline thanked the man, and he hastily made his exit. She sat close beside Ivy while she bravely opened the letter.

08 AUGUST 1942

THE SECRETARY OF WAR DESIRES ME TO EXPRESS HIS DEEP REGRET THAT YOUR HUSBAND PRIVATE FIRST CLASS HENRY WESTFIELD DIED OF WOUNDS RECEIVED IN ACTION STOP

PLEASE ACCEPT MY SINCERE SYMPATHY

THOMAS H LITTLEFIELD ADJUTANT GENERAL UNITED STATES ARMY

"Merciful God," uttered Caroline, bowing her head and weeping for Ivy.

Too stunned to move or speak, Ivy could think only of Lily and the fact that she would never know her father. She'd miss the thrill of having him teach her how to ride a bike, throw a ball, fish in the pond, or have him walk her down the aisle on her wedding day.

No tears came to Ivy's eyes. Instead, she immediately transformed into business mode, making mental lists of what she needed to do. Telling Hank's parents would be her first task. Next, plan a funeral and attend to the many arrangements that now fell to her. She stood erect, smoothed her dress, and walked back into the house with Caroline following close behind her.

"We will need to prepare the house, Caroline," she stated coldly. "I'm sure there will be many visitors."

Ivy's cool, calm reaction to the news concerned Caroline. She reasoned that shock must be the plausible cause for her actions, as she knew how much Ivy loved Hank.

It rained the day of Hank's funeral, making it difficult to discern the raindrops and the tears streaming down Ivy's face. Each shot fired from the gun salute assaulted her ears. As the bugler played "Taps," a white-gloved soldier knelt in front of Ivy and presented her with the folded American flag that had been draped over Hank's casket. Without looking up, Ivy accepted the flag.

Family members and friends gathered for the repast, a simple meal shared after the funeral, held at Ivy's house. When the last of the guests went home, Ivy retreated to her bedroom. She remembered nothing except the sight of the casket covered in bright red roses, as cemetery workers lowered it deep into the ground.

The days and weeks following the funeral seemed surreal. Ivy caught herself several times waiting for a letter from Hank, only to realize there would be no more. Seeing his clothes hanging in the closet tormented her, a reminder that he would never wear them again.

August 24, 1942

Dear Diary,

Fate has dealt a most dreadful hand. I have lost my one true love. I find myself trying desperately to recall the sound of Hank's voice, the glint in his eyes when he smiled, the feel of his gentle touch on my skin.

Lily is my only source of joy and comfort, and I see so much of Hank in her. I don't know what the future holds for us, but I'm determined to create a life for my daughter and me that Hank would be proud of. I pray for strength and wisdom.

Chapter Fourteen

Charleston, SC – 1942

Hank's father visited Ivy, bringing with him a letter that Hank had written shortly after arriving overseas. Hank held little optimism about returning from the war and made arrangements to ensure Ivy and Lily would be well taken care of for many years.

April 10, 1942

Dear Father,

I hope you and Mother are well. This war is very real and may continue for quite some time. I shall not go into the harsh details, but suffice it to say, I fear the worst. If something were to happen to me, please see to it that Ivy and Lily receive all the assets, savings, and insurance money they are entitled to from my accounts. You will find everything in order in the safe deposit box at the bank to which you hold the second key.

Please provide her guidance on monetary issues for both the immediate and distant future because she will need long-term financial support. If I may also ask, please be present in Lily's life in my absence and speak well of her father. Of course, my hope is that all this is for naught, and I will return home to my wife and child. Pray for all of us.

Your son,

Hank

While comforted by the knowledge that she'd be financially secure, Ivy struggled with being referred to as a "war widow." Thousands of other women, many from her own town, faced a future of uncertainty and loneliness.

As the number of widows grew in the county, so did Ivy's garden. She increased the amount of vegetables she grew so she could provide healthy food to those in need. She started raising chickens and a cow to supply them with fresh eggs and milk. In the fall, she canned vegetables. In the evenings, she crocheted blankets, sweaters, and hats, and distributed those as well. Ivy often hired unemployed men and women to lighten the load of tending to the garden and livestock. It helped ease the guilt she felt about having ample means to survive while others had so little.

November 1, 1942

Dear Diary,

Hank's been gone for several months now. The pain endures, but my chores keep my mind occupied. Unlike most other women, Lily and I are well provided for, but I try my best to teach her that it is better to give than to receive.

Caroline's husband, Walter, returned home after being wounded in action. The poor man had his leg amputated after stepping on a live grenade. Caroline hides her struggles while tending to his physical and emotional needs, but I know it is difficult for her. She brings Deidre to play with Lily, and they're becoming best pals. It is uplifting to see the innocence of their youth as they are oblivious to the tragedies happening around them.

One afternoon, Ivy received a letter in the mail. The envelope held something soft inside. She didn't recognize the name or address of the sender.

Carefully opening the letter, something fell onto her lap from inside the handwritten pages of the stationery. Ivy gasped in disbelief. It was the monogrammed handkerchief she had given to Hank before leaving for the service. *Where on earth did this come from?* Ivy read the letter.

November 12, 1942

Dear Mrs. Westfield,

Please allow me to introduce myself. My name is Alvin Hicks, and I'm from Chattanooga, Tennessee. Your husband Hank and I met aboard the ship that carried us to the South Pacific.

Although you and I have never met, I feel as if I know you through the stories Hank told me about you, your daughter, and your beautiful home in Charleston. Whenever he spoke of you, his eyes lit up with love and admiration. I felt it only proper to return the enclosed handkerchief to you. Hank never went anywhere without it and sometimes endured teasing from the other soldiers about carrying it with him. Please know it was all in good fun, as most of us held similar items in our own pockets.

Hank and I were together on the day of our platoon's attack. No one saw it coming, and we did our best to stay out of the line of fire. Hank found shelter but spotted a wounded soldier in the airfield and ran out to carry him back to safety. Hank saved the soldier's life but was shot from behind in the process. I ran to his side and discovered that he was gravely wounded. I managed to get him to the field hospital, but they were unable to save him. He clutched your handkerchief in his hand as he spoke his last words to me, "Tell Ivy I love her."

Please accept my deepest condolences for your loss. Hank was a hero and a good friend, and I'm proud to have known him. I wish you and your family Godspeed and pray for the end of this devastating war. Sincerely, Alvin Hicks, PFC

Ivy looked at the blood-stained handkerchief that Hank had held as he died. Until now, she hadn't broken down after receiving that fateful telegram from the War Department. She kept her composure and stood as a pillar of strength for Lily and all those around her, but this was too much to bear, and the floodgate of emotions finally broke wide.

She sobbed uncontrollably, and pain wracked her entire body. She cried for Hank, for the life they would never have together, and for Lily, who would grow up without her father. She cried for herself, now a young widow and single mother. She cried for all the other women bearing the same cross. The cathartic release left her emotionally depleted and physically exhausted. For the first time in months, she slept through the night without waking up in a cold sweat, reaching for Hank.

Charleston, SC – 1989

That night, Laney dreamt of soldiers, some still in their teens, falling in combat. The image of Ivy trying to comprehend the horrific news of Hank's death haunted her. Thoughts of her mother, fatherless like herself, ran through her mind. She awoke several times throughout the night before deciding to give up altogether. She made a strong cup of tea and waited for daylight to fill her bedroom.

At seven o'clock, she called Chase. He picked up the phone at once.

"Laney, what is it?" he asked with concern, since she was calling so early.

"Can you come over, Chase? I need someone to talk to."

She had barely hung up the phone when Chase came walking into the kitchen. He sat beside her at the table and asked, "What's wrong, Lane? Did something happen?"

"I've been reading more of my grandmother's diary and letters. She endured so much loss and tragedy but still managed to persevere and help others. My mother grew up not knowing her father, just like me. It's all so painful to think about."

"I know. The war played hell on most families. I'm sure many people appreciated all she did for them."

"She was an amazing woman. More so than I ever knew."

"Maybe you should take a break from reading her diary. I have a few errands to run in town today. Come with me, and we can go to the pier for lunch."

"That sounds wonderful."

"Okay, I'll be back around eleven to pick you up."

Chase went back home, and Laney showered and got dressed. Rascal followed closely at her heels all morning, as if he knew she was getting ready to leave.

"Don't worry, Rascal, I'll be back," she said as she threw one of his toys for him to fetch. She decided to wear a bright yellow sundress and arranged her long hair into a French twist. Chase arrived right on time. She grabbed her purse and met him outside. She noticed that he, too, was dressed a little nicer than usual.

"Don't you look handsome! I didn't realize our lunch date would be such a special occasion."

"You never know," he said with a mysterious tone in his voice.

It was a beautiful, sunny afternoon, and Laney welcomed the diversion as they drove into town. When Chase came to a stop on Main Street, he asked Laney to wait for him in the truck.

"I'll be back in a flash," he said, jumping out of the truck and disappearing down the street.

Laney couldn't see where he had gone but guessed he needed to pick up something for his dad. She listened to the mixtape of their favorite songs on the cassette player in the truck while waiting for him to return.

Chase reappeared a few minutes later. "Let's go," he said, as he backed out of the parking spot and headed toward the ocean.

Laney loved being close to the water and the beach. It soothed her soul and refreshed her frame of mind. "Chase, this is perfect," she exclaimed as she got out of the truck and breathed in the salty air. She pushed her sunglasses up into her teased hair, the wind tugging at the curls she'd sprayed into place that morning.

They walked to the restaurant and sat at an outdoor table overlooking the water. A small portable radio behind the bar played softly while noisy white seagulls circled overhead. They ordered lunch, and Chase seemed fidgety and a little nervous, quite out of character for him.

"Is something wrong, Chase?"

"No, of course not. Why do you ask?"

"No reason," she replied, thinking she must have imagined it.

As their drinks arrived, Chase turned to Laney and said, "You look beautiful today, Lane."

Laney smiled at his compliment, feeling a quiet warmth settle inside her and thanking him with a smile.

"It's a coincidence that you called me this morning because I was getting ready to call you."

"That's funny. Why were you calling?"

"To invite you to lunch today. I have something I need to talk to you about." He paused, and Laney waited patiently for him to continue.

"Laney, you know I'm a man of few words. You also know me well enough to understand that when I see something I want, I don't waste time getting it."

"Yes, that's true. But what are you getting at?"

"What I'm trying to say is, Lane," he began, as he took a small box out of his front pocket, "will you marry me?"

Laney stared at him, stunned as the meaning of his words slowly sank in.

"Say something, please."

"This is so sudden. Are you sure?"

"As sure as I know my own name. I love you, Laney, and want to spend the rest of my life with you." He took the ring out of the box and placed it on her finger.

Laney reached over to hug him. "I love you too, Chase."

"Is that a yes?"

"Yes, yes, yes," she exclaimed. "I will marry you!"

He kissed her and told her, "You've made me the happiest man on earth, Lane."

Several other diners at the tables around them heard his proposal and her acceptance and began to clap for them. Shouts of "congratulations" filled the air, and the waiter delivered a bottle of champagne, compliments of the house.

Laney couldn't stop gawking at the diamond ring on her finger. The exquisite setting consisted of a yellow gold band with a large round center stone surrounded by smaller diamonds.

"Chase, I love the ring you picked out. It's absolutely beautiful. Is that where you went today?"

"Yes, the jeweler called me last night and said it would be ready this morning."

Curious, Laney asked, "When did you order the ring?"

Chase admitted, "The day after we came home from New York. That's when I knew I never wanted to be without you."

After lunch, Chase and Laney went straight to his parents' house to share the happy news of their engagement. Mrs. Buchanan's keen sense of clairvoyance told her that the two of them were up to something.

"Don't you look pretty today, Laney!"

She stared at Laney and Chase, waiting for either one to say something. If the ear-to-ear smile on Laney's face didn't give away their secret, the shimmering diamond ring on her left hand as she held it up to Chase's mom surely did.

"It's official, Mrs. B—we're engaged!"

Mrs. Buchanan shouted for joy and drew Laney and Chase into an all-encompassing hug.

"Oh my goodness, this is wonderful news. I couldn't be happier for both of you." Marjorie had wished for this day for a long time; she always thought Laney was the perfect match for her son.

"Now you truly are my daughter, Laney!" she exclaimed, wiping a tear from her eye.

Chase's dad stepped inside with Buddy at his heels. The dog began jumping around the happy group, joining in the celebration.

"What's all the excitement?"

"Oh, Joe, soon we will have a new daughter!"

Joe was hardly surprised. Although he knew what she meant because Chase had discussed proposing to Laney with him last week, he couldn't pass up an opportunity to tease his wife a little.

"Marjorie, don't tell me you're pregnant!"

"No, of course not. Chase and Laney are engaged!"

They all broke out into riotous laughter.

"Congratulations, Laney," he said, hugging his soon-to-be daughter-in-law. "Welcome to the Buchanan family—though heaven knows you've already been part of this bunch practically your whole life."

That evening, Chase and Laney talked about their wedding plans and their future life together.

"Any idea when you want to get married?"

"I'll leave that up to you, Lane. Whenever and wherever is fine by me. Big or small, whatever you want."

Laney knew he meant it and would give her carte blanche to make the arrangements for the wedding. Chase only wanted one thing: to make Laney his wife. The details were immaterial to him, just as long as they were married. He did wonder about one thing, though.

"I assume you'll want to live here in your grandmother's house after we're married. Am I right?"

"I think so. This house means so much to me, and Ivy would have wanted that for us. Of course, it will need to be renovated and updated."

"We can do most of the renovations ourselves."

"Yes, we can remodel to our liking. It will make Ivy's home feel like our own, but I still want to keep a bit of her in every room."

"I like that idea! It's settled then; we'll live here."

He leaned over and kissed her, and she melted in his arms. Her solitary life in New York had been turned upside down in a matter of a month. Losing Ivy was devastating for her, but her pain and grief were softened by the anticipation of her marriage to her lifelong soulmate. Laney would have a home and a family of her own, the one thing she'd dreamed about since she lost her parents.

As Chase's kiss deepened, she was enraptured by feelings of love for him. She responded passionately as the electricity of his touch swept through her body like a tidal wave. Chase led Laney upstairs to her bedroom and closed the door. Gently lowering her onto the bed, he lay beside her. Laney closed her eyes and felt his lips travel from her face down her neck to her shoulder. His hands glided slowly down her sides before sliding beneath her blouse. Laney raised both arms and Chase lifted her shirt over her head, then he removed his. Before too long, they were completely undressed, their heated bodies entwined under the covers.

Laney was nervous and apprehensive because Chase was not only her first true friend, but also her first lover. Chase hesitated as he gazed into Laney's eyes.

"Laney, I want to make love to you, but if you aren't ready, we can stop."

"No, Chase, I want to. I love you."

"I love you too," he told her. Chase's hands lingered lovingly over her body. His tender caresses calmed her inhibitions, and she relinquished herself to him. Laney matched Chase's rhythmic movements as their lovemaking culminated with an overpowering intensity that bound them to each other forever. Afterward, they lay in each other's arms, sharing their newfound intimacy.

What started out as a day of sorrow and sadness ended with an engagement and the promise of a bright and happy future.

Chapter Fifteen

Charleston, SC – 1945

FROM THE TIME OF Hank's death until the end of the war, Ivy's diary entries were fewer and farther between. She raised Lily, ran the farm, and watched the world events as they unfolded.

In January 1945, President Roosevelt was inaugurated for an unprecedented fourth term in office. The president's health continued to fail, stemming in part from contracting polio as a child. On April 12, 1945, he died at his home in Warm Springs, Georgia. His body was transported by train back to Washington, DC. Throngs of grief-stricken citizens lined the tracks to pay homage to their beloved president as the train passed through their town, many saluting or covering their hearts with their hands.

Tragically, Franklin D. Roosevelt did not live to see World War II come to an end. On May 8, 1945, less than a month after his death, both the United States and Great Britain joyously celebrated Victory in Europe Day, or V-E Day. It was the end of a devastating war in which nearly sixty million people lost their lives, and millions more were injured.

People all over the world gathered in churches, on street corners, and in Times Square, New York, where ticker-tape parades were held to rejoice in the victory. For Ivy, the celebration was bittersweet. As she read the news reports of thousands of soldiers returning home to their families, she knew Hank would not be one of them. She found great comfort, however, in knowing that her brother and Hank's brother were on their way home. She wondered how the war had changed them and worried about their transition back to civilian life.

For Lily and Deidre, life went on. They started school together and remained close friends, often having sleepover parties at Ivy's house. They entered high school in September of 1954, and their friendship began to change over the next couple of years. They weren't compatible anymore and spent less time together. Ivy asked Lily about it one day and was taken off guard by her daughter's response.

"I haven't seen much of Deidre lately. Did you two have a falling out?"

"Mother," she shouted, "my friendships are none of your business! Keep out of my life!"

Lily stormed out of the house and didn't come back for several hours. Ivy had never heard Lily speak to her with such hatred and act so rebelliously. She began to question her ability to raise her. They had always been close, and Lily never let on that she was unhappy or discontented, so she assumed everything was fine.

Ivy called Caroline to see if she knew anything about what might be upsetting Lily. Caroline didn't want to lie to Ivy but struggled with a tactful way to tell her the truth about her daughter. Deidre had confided in her mother about Lily's changed personality in high school, particularly her relationships with boys.

"She is so different now. She flirts and runs off with older boys. I don't think she is promiscuous, but I know they drink beer, and I've seen her smoke cigarettes too. I just don't know who she is anymore," explained Deidre.

This new revelation shocked and saddened Caroline. She didn't want to hurt Ivy with this disturbing information about her daughter and thought it would be best to tell her in person. She wanted to be near her to console her. They met the next afternoon at Ivy's house.

"It's so good to see you." She ushered Caroline into the parlor, where Ivy had two glasses of iced tea ready. "How is Walter getting along?"

Caroline sighed and told her about the difficult time he had maneuvering with only one leg. "He just sits in his chair all day," she explained. "I think he could do a lot more, but he doesn't have any desire to. He's just a shell of the man I married."

Ivy felt bad for her friend. Deep down, she thought that her life without her husband was a fate much worse than Caroline had to endure. They talked a little more about inconsequential things as Caroline anxiously awaited the awkward discussion ahead of her.

"I know teenagers can be moody and awkward, but I didn't expect Lily's entire demeanor to change so drastically," she told Caroline. "Is it the same with Deidre?"

Caroline hesitated before answering; she didn't want to make it seem like her daughter was an angel. "They all have their moods, I guess. Deidre tends to be quiet and subdued. Lily has a zest for life."

Ivy pressed further. "Do you know what happened between the two girls?"

Caroline tried her best to explain the situation as gently and nonjudgmentally as possible. She struggled to find a delicate way to say that Lily was engaging in risky behavior. "Deidre told me that she'd rather not be around the same friends as Lily. I don't think Deidre is quite ready to have a boyfriend or, um..."

"Caroline, we're friends...you can tell me anything," Ivy pleaded.

"Well, Deidre doesn't drink, or smoke cigarettes, or stay out late with boys." There, Caroline said it aloud and hoped Ivy knew that she was implying that Lily did all those things without coming right out and accusing her. Ivy sat quietly in her chair for a moment.

"I think I understand what you're saying, Caroline," said Ivy. "I'm sure this must be very difficult for you, and I'm sorry if I pressured you to say more than you wanted to. You can certainly understand why I need to know."

"I do, Ivy, and I would want you to do the same for me."

They chatted for a little while longer, but Ivy's mind drifted a million miles away. She needed help rearing Lily if she wanted to keep her safe, and thought her brother Preston might be able to help her. She made a mental plan to talk to him soon. Caroline left shortly afterward, leaving Ivy alone with her thoughts.

May 12, 1957

Dear Diary,

Today I learned from Caroline that my daughter's behavior is less than respectable for a young lady. I had no idea of her interactions with boys and am shocked that she is on this path. I have only Preston to act as a father figure for Lily; however, I fear his angry and aggressive demeanor since returning from the war would not be helpful. I try to break through the wall she has erected between us, but nothing I do seems to help. I don't want to lose the closeness we have always shared, and I am genuinely concerned about where her actions will take her.

The more Ivy intervened in Lily's life, the more she pulled away. She tried to get her daughter involved in activities like helping with the church picnic, volunteering to tutor students after school, and even getting a summer job as a lifeguard since she loved to swim. None of these ideas were met with favor. Lily scoffed at her mother's feeble attempts to keep her away from her friends and let Ivy know about it.

"Mother, don't you think I see what you're doing? You can't stop me from being with my friends."

Ivy had taken just about enough of her daughter's sassiness and argued back, "You are my daughter, and I won't have you running all over town like some sort of tramp!"

Ivy surprised herself at her stern tone and accusations, but not nearly as astounded as Lily.

"What exactly are you saying, Mother?"

Ivy hoped she could snap some sense into Lily. "You run with boys, you smoke, you drink, and stay out late. Where do you think you'll end up if this sort of behavior continues?" she asked.

"The only way you would know all those things is if someone told you. Who was it? I bet it was Deidre."

"How I found out is not important," Ivy shot back, refusing to break Caroline's confidence. "Just know that I'm watching you and don't intend to sit back and let you ruin your life."

"I hate you, Mother!" Lily screamed as she ran out of the house.

Ivy followed her out into the yard and yelled back, "You may hate me now, but someday you'll thank me!"

It was no use; Lily ran off without even looking back. Every part of Ivy shook, and she went back into the house and lay down on the sofa, where she stayed for several hours, waiting for Lily to return. Ivy didn't realize she had fallen asleep until the first hint of daylight crept into the living room. She walked through the house calling Lily's name, but no one answered. She went into Lily's room and found that her bed had not been slept in. Ivy worried that she had caused Lily to run away and berated herself for what she had said the previous night. She picked up the phone and called her brother.

"Preston," she said in a desperate voice, "please come over right away."

Preston wasted no time getting to Ivy's house. He had never heard his sister sound as anxious and worried before.

"Ivy," he shouted as he entered the front door looking for her.

"I'm here, Preston, in the kitchen," she answered back. Ivy sat at the table, trying to calm her nerves with a cup of tea.

"What's going on?"

Ivy told him what had happened last night and asked Preston what he thought she should do. Preston wasn't sure he could help her since he was neither married nor had children of his own, but he offered to support Ivy in any way he could.

"It's clear that she isn't going to listen to what you tell her or any suggestions you give her to occupy her time. Maybe I should hang around the house a little more to show her a united front. Do you think that would help?"

"It couldn't hurt."

"First things first. We need to find her and bring her home."

Ivy didn't know where Lily went each time she left the house, so she called Caroline to see if Deidre could suggest a starting point to look for Lily. She put Deidre on the phone, who told Ivy that Lily often met up with her friends near the old bridge that connected Charleston to Mount Pleasant.

"Please don't tell her I told you," she begged.

Ivy promised she would keep her identity a secret, but knew that Lily would most likely figure it out.

"You're a good girl, Deidre, and you are doing Lily a great favor by helping us find her."

Preston and Ivy drove to the old bridge, where they found Lily with a group of boys and a few other girls. She had a cigarette dangling out of her mouth and a bottle of beer in her hand. Preston approached her.

"Lillian Spencer, come here right now."

Lily was mortified to see her uncle and embarrassed that he spoke to her as if she were a child. Her friends chided her.

"You'd better get home now, little Lily," one of them said to her.

"Shut up, Peter," Lily fired back. "I'm not going anywhere."

Ivy got out of the car and stood beside Preston. "Lily, get in this car, or I'll call the police and have them take you home."

Not wanting to make any more of a scene, Lily walked defiantly past her mother and uncle and got in the car. No one spoke the entire way home, but as soon as they got in the house, Lily started cursing the two of them for humiliating her in front of her friends. Preston put a stop to her barrage of hurtful insults directed at Ivy.

"Stop right there, little girl," he said sternly. "I will not have you talk to your mother like that. She's looking out for you and trying to keep you from making some mighty dangerous mistakes."

Lily shut her mouth but kept shooting daggers at Ivy, hate in her eyes.

"Now, apologize to your mother."

"For what? I didn't do anything."

"I hardly think drinking, smoking, and staying out all night are nothing at all, Lily. Your behavior is not going to be tolerated any longer. Apologize to your mother," he reiterated.

Lily realized they would not let up until she apologized. She made a half-hearted attempt at obliging her uncle's wishes.

"I'm sorry, Mother," she said quietly, avoiding eye contact with Ivy. "I'm going to my room now."

Later that afternoon, Ivy waited for Lily to get out of the shower and come downstairs. She hated the tension and discord between them and wanted to make things right. Lily finally appeared and greeted Ivy coolly but cordially.

"Hello, Lily. Are you hungry?"

"I can make my own lunch."

"Lily, I know you're upset with me, but please try to understand. I'm worried about your safety."

"I know, Mother."

Lily looked up at Ivy and noticed lines in her furrowed brow that had seemingly appeared overnight. Recognizing the worry she was causing her mother, Lily softened. She thought she should start helping more and to be less of a burden. But Lily suffered too. She never knew her father, and the only male figure in her life was her Uncle Preston, who was so grouchy all the time. She liked being around boys but didn't know how to act, so she just did whatever they wanted to do. Sometimes it didn't feel right, but she wanted so desperately to be accepted and loved by someone other than her mother.

"I'm sorry for the way I've been acting, Mom. I'll do better, I promise."

Ivy liked the sound of "mom" instead of "mother." She hugged Lily tightly and told her everything would be okay.

For a few weeks, Lily helped with the chores, accompanied Ivy to church on Sundays, and spent most of her free time at home. However, it didn't take long for Lily to become restless and bored. She missed her friends, no matter how bad their influence was on her.

While in town one day picking up groceries for Ivy, Lily heard someone shouting her name. She turned around and saw Peter Armstrong running across the street toward her.

"Where have you been, stranger?"

Lily was attracted to Peter, although she didn't know why. He was reckless, disheveled, and said more swear words than Lily had ever heard in her short life. Still, something about him intrigued Lily. Perhaps it was merely the fact that he paid attention to her when they were with their other friends.

"Hi, Peter. I've been staying close to home to help my mother."

"After what she did to you? I would have told my mother where she could go if she ever tried that with me."

Lily didn't appreciate his lack of respect for her mother but decided to overlook his crude remarks.

"Hey, wanna come down to the bridge tonight? We're all meeting there around eight."

"I'd better not, Peter," she said, rebuffing his invitation.

"Why not? Afraid your detective mother would track you down again?"

"It's not that, and please don't talk about my mother that way."

Peter knew he'd have to change his strategy if he wanted Lily to come out with him and his friends. He sidled up to her and put his arm around her shoulder.

"I really want to see you tonight, Lily. Please say you'll try to come."

Lily's heart raced when he touched her, and before she knew it, she told him she would find a way to sneak out of the house. His smile appeared genuine, but hiding behind it was a perverse satisfaction in how easily he could manipulate Lily.

Chapter Sixteen

Charleston, SC – 1989

Laney didn't hear Chase as he came through the back door into the kitchen. If it weren't for the commotion between Buddy and Rascal she wouldn't have even known he was in the house.

"Laney, are you here?"

Laney came running down the stairs to greet him. Still in her pajamas, she hadn't even showered yet.

"Good morning, Chase," she said as she stood on her tiptoes to give him a kiss.

"Morning?" he questioned. "It's almost one. What have you been doing all day? Did you forget we're meeting with the pastor at the church to talk about our wedding?"

Laney had no idea she'd been reading Ivy's diary for so long. "I'm sorry, Chase, I lost track of time."

"Let me guess...the diary again?"

"Yes, but please don't be angry with me. I'm getting to the part where my mother first met my father."

"Okay, but go get dressed or else we'll be late."

She hurried back upstairs, splashed water on her face, put her hair up in a ponytail with a scrunchie, and slipped into a sundress and sandals.

They arrived at the church on time and met with Pastor Stevens. A beige corded telephone sat on the corner of his desk beside a stack of printed church bulletins and a Rolodex. He had known them both since they were born and looked forward to joining them in matrimony. Laney and Chase wanted to keep the ceremony simple and agreed to have the traditional vows read.

After leaving the church, they went to the florist to pick out her bouquet, boutonnieres for Chase and his dad, and a corsage for his mother. Containers of carnations and baby's breath filled the shop, their sweet scents hanging in the warm air. It was nearing lunchtime, so they stopped at the local café for lunch. They sat at a booth by the window and ordered their food.

"I'm sorry for being a little impatient earlier, Lane."

"No, I'm sorry for not being ready on time. I'm learning so much about my mother; it's hard not to get wrapped up in reading the diary."

"I understand, really I do. I'd probably do the same thing if I were in your shoes."

After lunch, they went to purchase new cabinets and flooring for the kitchen. Chase flipped through a rack of vinyl flooring samples while Laney studied the cabinet finishes and Formica countertops. Starting there seemed logical since it was where they spent most of their time. Since the house would be under construction, Laney suggested the wedding ceremony be held at Chase's parents' house. Chase agreed, and so did the Buchanans.

"Don't worry about a thing, Laney. I'll take care of all the details," said Marjorie.

"Thank you! That takes a lot of work off my plate."

"What else do you have going on, dear?"

"Besides the renovations Chase and I are working on, I'm meeting with Deidre later this week to talk about my mother."

"I hope that goes well. If you need someone to talk to afterward, I'll be here."

"I appreciate that...more than you know." Laney felt blessed to be part of this amazing family and couldn't wait to officially become a Buchanan.

That Friday, Deidre met Laney at the house. For Deidre, it was a sentimental journey back to her childhood. She had so many memories of playing with Lily and learning about life on a farm. She'd enjoyed being outside in the fresh air instead of staying cooped up in the small apartment where she lived with her parents. She and Lily had some wonderful times together; however, not all the memories were good ones.

During high school, Deidre and Lily's friendship ended abruptly, which caused her great anguish and regret. She adored Lily and hated the fact that her self-destructive behavior eventually ended her life. Deidre often wondered if she could have done something to stop her from getting involved with Peter Armstrong, but Lily was too strong-willed to listen to reason.

"Thank you for coming over today. I can't tell you how much it means to me to talk with someone who was as close to my mother as you were."

"You're welcome, Laney. I don't know what I can tell you about her that you don't already know, but I'll do my best."

"That's just it... I really don't know much at all, except for the little my grandmother said about her and what I learned from Ivy's letter to me after she died. I would appreciate whatever you can tell me."

Deidre wanted to be as delicate and discerning as possible. The look of hope and longing in Laney's eyes told her it would be difficult to soft-soap the truth.

Deidre began talking about her relationship with Lily. "We were practically like sisters, both the same age and together all the time. We liked the same things and never argued. We both styled our hair in ponytails, wore poodle skirts with bobby socks and saddle shoes, and bright red lipstick when our moms weren't looking. We were in love with Elvis, Fabian, and Ricky Nelson."

Deidre hesitated a bit as she wistfully recalled the memories of she and Lily listening to their favorite records on the phonograph.

"We learned all the new dances and loved going to sock hops. Those carefree years were so much fun."

"It all sounds so wonderful."

"Indeed. Lily was always the life of the party and up for anything."

"What happened between you two?"

Deidre knew the time had come to tell Laney the details about how she and Lily had parted ways. "Your mom matured a little faster than I did during our high school years," she explained as gracefully as possible. "I wasn't yet as attracted to boys as Lily, and we hung around with a different circle of friends."

Deidre watched Laney's reaction as she continued, "Lily liked one boy in particular, your dad, Peter Armstrong. He didn't care much for me, and Lily had to make a choice between Peter and her old friend. Unfortunately, there wasn't room for both of us in her life, and we drifted apart."

"I'm so sorry, Deidre. I'm sure it must have been painful to lose your best friend."

"Yes. By the time we graduated high school, we rarely saw each other. I heard bits and pieces about her life through your grandmother, including when she married your father. I always imagined we would stand as maids of honor in each other's weddings, but it never happened."

Deidre stopped talking, her eyes glistening with tears. Until today, she hadn't realized how much she had missed her childhood friend.

Laney handed Deidre a tissue.

"I'm sorry, Laney. I loved her so much and miss her terribly." She took a moment to compose herself.

"Maybe it would be best if we stopped, at least for today."

"Perhaps we can meet another time," Deidre offered. "You have a lot going on with the wedding plans, and I don't want to upset you with stories of the past that can't be rewritten."

Laney thanked Deidre for visiting, and they promised to meet again soon.

Chase came over a few hours later and asked Laney how things had gone with Deidre. The look in her eyes told him all he needed to know.

"Rough day, Lane?" he asked, putting his arm around her and gently kissing her temple.

"Yes, quite emotional, but I'm glad Deidre and I had the chance to talk."

"Did you learn anything new?"

"Only a little about what my mother was like in school, but not much else. We plan to meet after the wedding."

Chase sensed Laney's frustration and feared they might never uncover all the details about what actually happened almost thirty years ago.

"The wedding is only eight days away. Why don't we put this on the back burner for now so you can concentrate on our special day?"

Laney wanted to disagree with Chase and continue her relentless journey to find the answers to the questions burning within her, but the look in his eyes changed her mind. He looked so sincere and concerned about her that she didn't have the heart to argue. This mystery wasn't going anywhere, and another week wouldn't change any of the facts.

"You're right," she relented. "I want our wedding day to be perfect. All this can wait."

Charleston, SC – 1989

CHASE AND LANEY CONTINUED working to finish as many of the renovations as they could before the wedding. The kitchen and dining rooms were almost done, leaving only the upstairs rooms to be completed. Since Ivy's room was the largest of the three bedrooms, it seemed logical to use it as theirs. They moved her furniture into the empty bedroom at the east end of the hallway. Chase slapped a fresh coat of paint on the walls and fixed the broken windowsill. On Thursday, a new bed, dresser, and two nightstands that they had ordered from a furniture catalog were delivered. Laney bought a new quilted bedspread and hung matching curtains in the windows, adding a fresh touch.

The time had come for new memories to be made. Laney managed to keep Chase out of the house the day before the wedding. She wanted everything to be just right for their first night home as husband and wife.

On Saturday, September 18, 1989, the big day arrived. As Laney began preparing for her wedding, she reflected on all the changes in her life over the past six months. Losing Ivy, reconnecting with Chase, moving to Charleston, and now getting married to her best friend overwhelmed Laney, and she became emotional. She wished her grandmother were here to witness their wedding and be part of this special day.

Marjorie came over to help Laney get ready and sensed the melancholy in the room. "I think I know what's going through your mind, Laney," she said as she sat beside her at the dressing table. "Do you want to talk about it?"

Laney rested her head on her shoulder. Marjorie stroked her arm and said, "Ivy loved you more than anything, and she's with you today in spirit."

"Thank you," Laney said, wiping a tear with her linen handkerchief. "I feel her presence too."

"That's a beautiful handkerchief, Laney. Where did you get it?"

"I found it while reading my grandmother's letters from World War II. She gave it to my grandfather to carry with him for comfort while he was away from her. I thought it would be special to carry a piece of both of them with me today."

"That is so touching, Laney. She would have loved that."

Marjorie smiled sweetly and helped Laney tease and spray the soft curls around her face before fastening the row of small buttons on the back of her wedding dress. Laney was so grateful they had time alone to share this tender moment. If her own mother couldn't be present to spend this special occasion with her, she could think of no one else she would rather have there than Chase's mom.

The wedding of Laney and Chase was an intimate affair. Laney wore an elegant white linen, three-quarter-length dress and a delicate gardenia pinned in her hair. Chase wore a black suit and a tie and waited under the trellis in the Buchanan's backyard, where simple white ribbons had been tied among the vines. Chase's family and a few of their friends sat in chairs set up on the lawn.

At dusk, a member from Marjorie's church played the wedding march softly on the violin to begin the ceremony. Chase's dad hooked arms with Laney, and they proceeded toward the makeshift altar. He kissed her on the cheek and led her to Chase's side. Awestruck by her beauty, he had no words. They turned to face Pastor Stevens, who began, "Dearly beloved, we are gathered here today to celebrate the union of Laney Armstrong and Chase Buchanan. I've known these two wonderful people their whole lives and couldn't be happier to join them together in holy matrimony."

The setting sun created a hazy, romantic backdrop as the couple recited their vows to each other.

Laney began first. "I, Laney Armstrong, take you, Chase Buchanan, to be my lawfully wedded husband..."

Chase continued with his part. "...to have and to hold, in sickness and in health, for richer or poorer, 'til death do us part."

They exchanged rings, and Pastor Stevens declared, "I now pronounce you husband and wife."

They shared their first kiss and turned to greet their guests as Mr. and Mrs. Chase Buchanan. Afterward, they enjoyed a light supper, and Chase's dad toasted their union.

"To Chase and Laney," said Joe Buchanan with a raised glass of champagne, "I wish you both a lifetime of love and happiness."

Marjorie joined in and added, "May peace and contentment be with you always. Let joy fill your lives as you continue the Buchanan family name for generations to come."

Filled with elation, Laney belonged to this family now and was proud to be a Buchanan. She wiped a tear with Ivy's handkerchief and said a silent prayer of thanks.

They danced together as husband and wife to their favorite song, "I Only Have Eyes for You," as their guests watched and a friend of Chase's recorded the scene on his camcorder.

During the evening, Chase introduced Laney to some of his relatives she hadn't met yet.

"Laney, this is my dad's Uncle Billy," he said as the two greeted his elderly great-uncle sitting in a wheelchair. "He didn't want to miss the wedding of his only great nephew, so my dad picked him up this morning from the nursing home in West Ashley."

"It's a pleasure to meet you, sir. I'm so glad you could come."

"Hold on a minute there, little darlin'," said Uncle Billy, vigorously shaking Laney's outstretched hand. "None of that 'sir' stuff. I'm your uncle now, too."

All three of them laughed, and Laney promised to call him Uncle Billy.

"Chase mentioned that you knew my Uncle Preston."

At the mention of Preston Spencer, Uncle Billy's jovial kidding changed to a more somber tone. "Sure, but it was a long time ago."

Laney made a mental note to visit him at a later date, hoping he might fill in some of the missing details about her father. But for now, she wanted to enjoy the remainder of the night.

Chase and Laney cut their two-tiered, rose-decorated wedding cake. They fed each other the traditional first piece before cutting the rest to serve to their guests. The joyous event continued until around nine. Mrs. Buchanan promised to take care of the wedding gifts, adding that Chase and Laney could come by the next day to open them.

Exhausted, the couple said their goodbyes before heading back to their house.

"Thank you for making our day so special, Mrs. B."

"You're welcome, Laney dear. And please, if you would like to, call me Mom."

Laney's heart swelled, and she hugged Marjorie affectionately. She looked into her mother-in-law's eyes and said, "I would love to, Mom."

"That goes for me, too. I mean, you can call me Dad, not Mom."

Always awkward in sentimental moments, Mr. B's joke was meant to lighten the mood. But even he became caught up in the joy they all felt as Laney rushed into his arms.

"Thank you, Dad, for everything. I will always treasure our walk down the aisle as one of the happiest moments of my life."

Chase and Laney walked home to begin their new life together. The house at 5037 Cypress Lane was their home now. Love and laughter would once again ring throughout the house, just as Ivy and Hank intended, so many years ago.

As Laney put the key in the front door to enter the house, Chase stopped her from going inside.

"Mrs. Buchanan. Please allow me the honor of carrying you over the threshold."

Touched by his romantic gesture, she let him lift her off her feet into his arms. Together, they glided through the door into the parlor. He kissed her neck before lowering her to the floor.

"I like hearing you call me Mrs. Buchanan."

"Get used to it, Mrs. Buchanan," he repeated, noticing how her eyes sparkled at the sound of her new name.

He led her upstairs to their newly decorated bedroom. Earlier that morning, Laney had covered the bed in rose petals and scented the sheets with lavender. As they prepared for bed, she lit a candle on each of their nightstands, and the flickering light washed the room with a soft amber glow.

Chase stood behind her and slowly unfastened the buttons of her dress, letting it slip off her slender hips onto the floor. Laney unbuttoned his shirt and pushed it back over his broad shoulders. She closed her eyes as he kissed her passionately.

"I love you, Laney."

"I love you too, Chase," she responded breathlessly.

Laney had everything she always wanted: a husband, a best friend, and a soulmate with whom she would spend the rest of her life. Their lovemaking transcended her into a state of blissful happiness she had never known. She felt as if the two of them had become one, never to be separated.

The next morning, Chase got up first and prepared breakfast to serve Laney in bed.

"Do you think it will always be like this, Chase?"

"I can't guarantee breakfast every morning."

"No, silly, that's not what I meant. I mean this head-over-heels, crazy-in-love feeling."

"I certainly hope so."

They lingered in bed for a while, enjoying the closeness and newness of being married. They stayed there until Rascal started fussing outside the bedroom door, waiting to be fed.

"Looks like he has other plans for us this morning, Lane."

"He's like a little kid wanting our attention. Guess we'd better see to him before he knocks down the door."

Chase opened the bedroom door, and Rascal bounded up on the bed, smothering Laney in wet kisses. The breakfast tray toppled to the floor, sending muffin crumbs in every direction.

Chase asked Laney, "Do you think it will always be like this, Lane?"

They both started laughing, and Laney replied, "I certainly hope so."

They spent the rest of the day in blissful leisure, strolling past the pond and relaxing outside. In the evening, they went to the Buchanans' to open their wedding gifts. There were plenty of leftovers from the reception, so they didn't need to cook dinner that night.

The next day, it was business as usual. Chase went to his dad's to work, and Laney continued working on the house. They had decided to postpone the honeymoon until the house was completely finished and they could truly relax.

While rummaging through the attic, Laney found the bassinet that had been her mother's. Still in good condition, it could be used again, if and when the circumstances arose. Laney also found a collection of Lily's baby clothes and toys, along with a scrapbook containing a snippet from her first haircut and the first lost baby tooth. A dried red rose was pressed between the pages of the book with a note beside it that read, "To my wife and mother of my daughter. Love, Hank."

Laney envisioned Hank and Ivy cooing and fussing over their firstborn daughter with dreams of a houseful of children. It saddened her that the loss of her husband changed the direction of Ivy's life. She never remarried after Hank died, noting in her diary that he was her one true love and no other man could take his place. Laney felt the same way about Chase. He was all she ever wanted and hoped they would live long and happy life together.

"Lane, are you up there?" she heard Chase call out from the parlor. He climbed up the narrow stairway to the attic and found her sitting on the floor among the trunkful of baby things.

"What's all this?" he asked, holding up one of Lily's frilly little dresses.

Laney's face reddened, hoping Chase didn't think she was hinting at starting a family right away. "Just some things of my mother's that Ivy saved. I found them inside this old trunk of hers. Don't look so worried. I can assure you I'm not entertaining any thoughts of having a baby, at least not right now."

Laney thought he would be relieved, but Chase's reply surprised her. "Why not, Lane? Don't you want a family?"

"Of course I do. But don't you think it's a little too soon? After all, we've been married less than a week!"

"I guess you're right, Lane, but it's a nice thought that someday we will fill this big old house with a few little Buchanans."

"Yes, we will. Ivy would be so happy that her great-grandchildren continued her legacy."

"I'm going to the hardware store for a few things. Do you want to come along?"

"No thanks. I think I'll catch up on reading the diary. I haven't turned a page since before the wedding, and I'm anxious to continue where I left off."

"Okay. I'll be back in about an hour or so," he said. He kissed her forehead and went back downstairs, but not before teasing her once more. "Don't go setting up that bassinet until I return."

She picked up a pillow and launched toward him, narrowly missing his head as he scooted down the steps. "I'll try to contain myself!" she shouted after him in amusement.

Chapter Eighteen

Charleston, SC – 1957

M UCH TO IVY'S DISMAY, she learned that her daughter had been secretly meeting Peter Armstrong. While picking up a few things at the store, she overheard the stockboy telling his friend that Peter Armstrong was a smooth talker. He detailed how Peter had convinced his "girlfriend" to lie to her mother and meet him at the river after dark last night.

June 2, 1957

Dear Diary,

Lily has been lying to me about her whereabouts. She told me she went to a friend's house to study. Instead, she sneaked off to meet that boy, Peter Armstrong. I can't seem to control her and am afraid she will do something rash. I don't want to scare her away by being too strict, but I cannot sit back and watch her be led down the wrong path.

Lily felt pressured from all sides. Her mother wouldn't believe her fabricated tales of being at the library with a friend or babysitting a neighbor's children much longer. Eventually, she would get caught.

Peter pressed hard for her to meet him more often. He made demands of her time and tried to persuade Lily to do things with him she'd never done before. She hadn't even kissed a boy, and hated it when Peter started groping her. She made it very clear to him that she wasn't "that" kind of girl. He backed down and would be patient if, in the end, he got what he wanted.

Ivy confided in Preston about Lily's lying and staying out late. He took it upon himself to investigate Peter Armstrong and asked some of his friends around Charleston about him. He started by paying a visit to his friend Billy Buchanan.

"Preston, old buddy, what brings you out to these parts?"

"Hey, Billy, got a minute?" asked Preston.

"Sure, I've always got time for a friend." Billy welcomed Preston into his house and offered him a beer.

"No thanks. It's a little too early in the day for me."

"What can I do for you?"

Preston got straight to the reason for his visit. "What do you know about that kid, Peter Armstrong? He's been hanging around my niece, and my sister Ivy is concerned about it."

"I can't say that I blame her. That boy's been on his own since his mama left his daddy when he was a baby. I guess she'd had enough of his drinking and carousing, and took off. His daddy left him alone most of the time. If it weren't for the few friends and neighbors who lived nearby, Petey would scarcely have had anything to eat."

"I remember seeing his father being thrown out of a bar in town for drinking and not paying his bill," recalled Preston.

"Sounds about right. Then he'd go home and beat the kid for something he did. It wasn't until Petey's teachers noticed the bruises on his face and arms that he got taken away and sent to a foster home."

"Sounds like a tough life for a kid."

"Yeah, it sure was. I couldn't help but feel sorry for him. He moved around from one home to another until no one would take him in. He dropped out of school and went back to live with his father. It wasn't the best situation, but at least he had a roof over his head. He learned to stay out of his daddy's way whenever he got drunk."

"Whatever happened to his father?"

"One day, Petey came home to find him on the garage floor, a pool of blood surrounding his gashed head. He'd fallen off a ladder reaching for his hidden stash of moonshine and met his maker."

"I guess Peter was old enough to live on his own by that time," said Preston.

"Yeah. Petey was neither sad nor sorry to see the cold, stiff corpse of his daddy lying on the ground. Now he could come and go as he pleased. He started robbing local stores and homes for money to survive. He spent time in jail at least five times before his eighteenth birthday."

"I can't understand why Lily would want to be within ten feet of a boy like Peter."

"He may be a snake in the grass, but he's also a charmer. I'd keep my eye on him if I were you, Preston."

"I plan to do that, Billy. Thanks for the tip. I owe you one."

"Heck, after all you've done for me, saving my hide overseas like you did, I'd say the scales are tipped in your favor."

"Nah. Your hide was worth saving. If there's one thing I can't stand, it's one of my friends getting pushed around. You take care of yourself."

"You too, pal."

Preston needed to find a way to dissuade Lily from seeing Peter, if not for her own safety, then for Ivy's sake. Ivy didn't deserve to be lied to and deceived by her own daughter for this no-good hoodlum.

Preston waited in front of Lily's school one afternoon to catch her before she started walking home. When he spotted her heading toward a group of her friends, he jogged over to greet her.

Surprised to see her uncle at her school, Lily greeted him and asked, "Uncle Preston, what are you doing here?"

He asked if she wanted to join him for an ice cream at the local diner. Although skeptical about his invitation, she didn't refuse in case Ivy had sent him to monitor her whereabouts. "Sure, I'd love to," she lied.

Lily fidgeted in the booth opposite her uncle, trying to guess why he wanted to talk with her. He made her uncomfortable, especially when his anger surfaced. His voice could become loud and aggressive even during the most benign conversations with her mother. Ivy explained that his time in the Army made him that way. Lily always tried to make herself scarce whenever he came to the house to visit.

"What'll you have?" asked the waitress standing next to their table.

"Lily, you first."

"I'll have a chocolate malted, please."

"Same here," Preston told the waitress.

Lily let her gaze wander around the diner, purposefully avoiding Preston's steady stare.

"Lily, I want to talk to you about your mother. She's been worried about you, and I don't like seeing her this upset."

"Did she send you to talk to me?"

"No, she didn't. I came of my own volition because I'm trying to help. She loves you, Lily. It isn't easy for her to raise a young daughter by herself."

Without skipping a beat, Lily retorted, "It isn't easy for me either, not having a father."

Preston didn't want to enter into a spitting match with his niece and tried to de-escalate the situation. "I understand, Lily."

"Do you really, Uncle Preston? How could you possibly know what it's like for me?"

Seeing how agitated she had become, he thought perhaps this wasn't the best idea. The waitress delivered their drinks to the table, giving them a welcome break in the conversation. Lily sipped her malted through the striped straw, hoping this little tête-à-tête would end soon. Preston chose his words carefully so as not to upset Lily even more.

"As your uncle, you can always come to me, Lily, if you ever need advice or someone to talk to."

Lily wasn't interested in anything her uncle had to say, but didn't want to make him even more suspicious. The last thing she needed was both her mother and her uncle breathing down her neck.

"Thank you, Uncle Preston," she said in the sweetest voice she could muster. "I'll keep that in mind."

Preston sensed she was pacifying him, but decided to let it go for now. He would keep a watchful eye on both Lily and Peter as discreetly as possible. His niece was a good girl most of the time, but she could be sneaky and deceptive at other times.

The waitress brought the check, and Preston laid down a five-dollar bill on the table. They walked outside together, and

Lily spotted Peter across the street. Her uncle was facing the opposite direction and didn't see him.

"Thanks for the malted, Uncle Preston. I'm going over to the library now to study for a while before going home."

"Can I give you a lift, Lily?"

"No, it's just around the corner. I can walk."

Preston let her go, but the raised hair on the back of his neck told him she had lied to him. His suspicions were confirmed when he turned and caught a glimpse of Peter across the street, walking in the same direction as Lily. They both walked into the library, so Preston hung around outside for a while.

Lily's hands shook as she pulled a random book from the shelf. She scurried over to a secluded table in the far corner of the room, pretending to be interested in the book. A minute or two later, Peter appeared and took a seat next to her.

"Hello, beautiful. Is everything okay?"

"I think I'm being watched," she said nervously as she glanced around the room. Peter scanned the room too, but didn't see anyone who looked out of the ordinary.

"Who's watching you?"

"My mother and my uncle Preston, that's who."

"Oh, you mean the guy I saw you with outside the diner?"

"Yes. I think my mother sent him after me, even though he said she didn't know about it."

"Don't worry about it until you have to," said Peter as he reached under the table and rested his hand on her knee. Lily jumped at the touch of his hand and nearly dropped the book. Peter found delight in knowing he had such an effect on her.

"Why did you want to meet me?"

"I need a favor from you, sweetheart," he said, slowly moving his hand up the length of her thigh.

"Peter, stop that! Not here," she scolded him. Peter backed off a little but sensed his closeness rattled her.

"Lily, I need to borrow some money. I need about fifty dollars."

"Fifty dollars! Are you crazy?" she shouted.

"Shush. Do you want to get us thrown out of here?"

They both looked up to see the gray haired librarian shooting them scalding looks that meant either keep quiet or leave.

"Why would you think I have that kind of money?"

"Your mother is loaded, Lily, surely you have some too."

"Whatever gave you that idea? The answer is no!"

Lily couldn't believe his request. *Is Peter only using me for money?*

Peter sidled up to her, put his arm around the back of her chair, and said, "Not even for your boyfriend, Lily?"

Lily found it incredibly difficult to keep her reserve with Peter so close, but this time, she wouldn't back down. "It's not that, Peter, it's just that I don't have any money, and I have no idea where my mother keeps hers."

Peter tried a different tactic in hopes that she'd change her mind. "Okay, Lily," he said coldly, removing his arm from the back of her chair. "I thought I meant more to you than that. Maybe you don't want me as your boyfriend anymore."

His words were calculating and devious, meant to hurt Lily. No other boys were interested in her, mostly because he scared them all away with threats of harm if one of them looked in her direction. He pressed on, "Maybe I'll have to find a new sweetheart."

Peter broke off all eye contact with Lily and let his last statement linger in the air while he waited for her to cave in. It took less time than he thought it would, and he was quite pleased with himself.

"No, Peter, please," she begged him. "I'm your girlfriend. I'll find a way to get the money."

"That's better. Now, let's not leave at the same time in case your uncle is lurking around. You go out first through the front door, and I'll duck out the back door."

Preston watched Lily come out of the library alone and hoped she'd been studying like she had told him she was. He left without her noticing he was spying on her and reported his meeting with Lily to Ivy. He reassured his sister that she could count on him to be a male figure in Lily's life. Ivy thanked her brother, grateful for his support.

"I don't know what I would do without you, Preston. Life is hard for a woman alone, and sometimes Lily can be a handful."

"Don't worry, sis, I'm here to help you. I'll try to stay a bit closer to the house from now on so Lily can see there's someone here besides you to look out for her."

Lily hadn't even realized she'd walked all the way home until she found herself standing in front of the house. She had never stolen anything in her life...and certainly not from her own mother. She hated herself for even thinking about taking her mother's money to keep Peter as her boyfriend.

Still...Peter listened to her when no one else would, even though sometimes he didn't pay attention to what she said. He made her feel wanted and loved, at least some of the time. No other boys in her class looked at her, and she didn't know why.

Lily wished she still had Deidre as a friend to confide in. She needed someone level-headed and rational to talk to. But she and Deidre had drifted apart earlier in the year because of Peter. Sometimes Lily didn't think he was worth it, but no one else cared about her.

Ivy paid the men who worked for her every Friday. She paid them in cash and kept the money in a strong black metal box locked in her bedroom closet. Prudent with her money, Ivy would know if any were missing, especially a large amount like fifty dollars. Lily thought she might be able to take a little at a time, so it wouldn't be missed, but decided that wouldn't work either. Ivy kept a detailed ledger of her income and expenses in ink, making the entries impossible to alter. She had to think of something else.

While Ivy tended to the garden, Lily wandered into her mother's bedroom. She remembered Ivy telling her that before her father died, he gave her very expensive gifts, including jewelry, which she seldom wore anymore. Lily peeked inside

Ivy's jewelry box and rifled through its contents. There were rings, bracelets, brooches, and a gold locket that Lily had never seen. *This should be worth at least fifty dollars, if not more.* She turned it over and read the engraved inscription on the back: "I will love you until the end of time. Hank."

A tear escaped from Lily's eye when she read the words her father had written to her mother. The date read April 6, 1940—their wedding day. *No! I cannot take this and sell it, for I would hate myself for all eternity.*

Ivy called out to Lily as she approached the bedroom. Lily slammed the drawer shut and ran out of the room, bumping right into her mother.

"Lily, dear, what's the matter?"

"Nothing, Mother, I'm fine."

"But sweetheart, you're crying. Something must be wrong."

Realizing what she had almost done jolted Lily. She yearned to be comforted and reassured that she wasn't an evil girl who would rob from her own mother. "I love you, Mom," Lily told Ivy, meaning it for the first time in a while.

"Oh, my sweet girl, I love you too. Is there something you want to tell me?"

Lily needed to purge her soul, thinking it would somehow rid her of the hold Peter Armstrong had over her.

"I'm so sorry," Lily said, sobbing into her mother's bosom. "I've been acting like a spoiled brat. Can you please forgive me?"

Ivy rocked her daughter in her arms like she had when Lily feared thunder and lightning during a storm as a child. "Of course, Lily. What have I always told you?"

They both repeated the phrase that Ivy had been telling Lily her whole life: "God doesn't have a limit on how many times he forgives us, and neither do I."

"Thank you, Mom. I don't deserve you."

"Nonsense. You're the best daughter a mother can have."

June 10, 1957

Dear Diary,

The miracle I've been praying for has happened; my Lily has come back to me. I'm so happy to share special moments with my baby girl once again. I'll most likely never learn what led to her transformation, but that is of no importance as long as she is back in my arms. Life is good again.

In June 1958, Lily graduated from high school. In an effort to change, she took her mother's advice and became a lifeguard at the local swimming club for the summer. She also led art courses and enjoyed encouraging the children to explore their creativity. It was a welcome departure from hanging around with her old friends and getting into trouble.

Lily stayed close to home, trying her best to avoid Peter. She thought she was rid of him until he cornered her one day coming out of the grocery store.

"Where've you been hiding, Lily? How come I haven't seen you around?"

"I've been busy working," she said matter-of-factly as she walked away from him.

Peter pressed her further. "I've missed you," he said, trying his old tricks to sweet-talk her.

Lily stood her ground. "Look, Peter, I don't want to see you anymore. Please leave me alone."

"But Lily, wait a minute. I just want to talk to you."

Fortunately for Lily, Uncle Preston came out of the store right behind her. He witnessed the exchange between Lily and Peter and quickly intervened.

"Is there a problem here, Lily?"

Peter retreated at once. Lily knew she'd made the right decision to always go to town accompanied either by her mother or her uncle.

"No problem, Uncle Preston," she said, as they proceeded to his car to return home. She planned to stay as far away from Peter Armstrong as possible.

As summer was coming to a close, Ivy wondered about Lily's future plans. Deidre was leaving for college in the fall to study to become a teacher. Lily hadn't mentioned wanting to continue her education, even though Ivy assured her that her tuition would be paid for whatever college she'd choose to attend. She liked the fact that Lily stayed home more often, but wanted more for her only daughter. She was a smart young woman with a bright and promising future ahead of her.

"Lily, have you given any thought about what you would like to do now that school is out?"

Lily's interests were in fashion and clothing design. She had a good eye for style and a talent for combining colors and textures to create stunning outfits. She considered attending the Art Institute of South Carolina but doubted her readiness for such a large undertaking.

"I've been toying with a few ideas. What would you think of me applying to an art school?"

"I think that's a wonderful idea!"

"Really? Do you think I would be accepted?"

"Of course I do, but you'll never know unless you apply. Let's visit a few schools and make a plan."

Lily sent in an application and got accepted to art school. She spent the next four years studying color, fabric, and dress design, filling sketchbooks with ideas and learning how to drape cloth across dress forms and turn patterns into finished garments. By the time she graduated, at the top of her class, she had developed a keen eye for style and proportion.

Soon after, she was hired as an associate designer for a fashionable dress shop in Charleston. Her days were spent among bolts of wool crepe and printed cotton, measuring tapes draped around her neck as she helped sketch and fit slim sheath dresses and tailored suits for the shop's customers. Many of the women who came through the door arrived in pearls and white gloves, their hair styled in careful bouffants before an afternoon of shopping.

Lily found a small apartment only a few blocks from the shop. She wasn't especially fond of the harvest gold shag carpet, but she overlooked it in exchange for the convenience of being able to walk to work past the storefront windows along King Street. Even with her busy schedule, she made time to visit Ivy often, helping with chores around the house and lingering over coffee at the kitchen table whenever she could.

July 18, 1962

Dear Diary,

It makes a mother proud to see her child flourish and grow. Lily is successful and happier than I've seen her in a long time. This big house seems empty without her living here, but she visits often, which is all I can ask for. Perhaps, one day, she will marry and have children of her own, and the circle of life will continue.

Lily hadn't given Peter Armstrong a second thought in years until one day in late August, their paths crossed. She spent a good portion of her days and evenings working hard and needed a break. She took an afternoon off and went to the beach to relax and soak up the sun. While aimlessly walking along collecting seashells, she heard someone call her name. She turned around and saw a man coming toward her who looked a lot like Peter except for the long hair. She shielded her eyes from the bright sun and recognized his face.

"Peter?" she said in total surprise at seeing him there.

"Lily? I thought that was you," he said, his breath ragged from running to catch up with her. "How are you?"

"I'm good, Peter. How about you?"

They walked and talked for a while. Lily learned that he had left town for a few years to work for a friend in West Virginia, but returned to Charleston to work on the docks. She told him about her new career and mentioned that she lived on her own. This news piqued Peter's interest.

"I've thought about you a lot lately, Lily."

"Really," she said flatly. It wasn't a question but a statement of skepticism.

"Sure, I thought we really had something special, you and me."

Lily wasn't in the mood to argue with him. She wanted to enjoy her day off without any worries. Peter looked at his watch and realized his lunch break ended ten minutes ago.

"Well, I gotta run. Maybe I'll see you again sometime soon."

"Goodbye, Peter," she said noncommittally.

Suddenly, she didn't want to stay there anymore. Lily walked back to her blanket, gathered her things, and headed back home. She decided to spend the rest of the afternoon getting lost in a good book.

Peter couldn't believe his luck at running into Lily on the beach. He'd only been back in town a few weeks and was tired of sleeping in his car. He hated loading and unloading heavy cargo from ships. It was back-breaking work for very low pay. He was ready to throw in the towel and try something else when Lily appeared. She was established, successful, and—not to mention—would likely inherit a considerable sum of money someday.

Peter went to the YMCA to shower and clean up. He got a haircut and bought new clothes to look more presentable. He planned to be on his best behavior in hopes of getting Lily back.

Lily's job proved to be quite rewarding. Her boss appreciated her artistic ability and fine attention to detail, and promoted her to assistant designer. For a young woman just beginning her career, it was an opportunity few received so quickly. The two worked closely together, and Lily began designing items for their signature line of women's wardrobe. She loved her job and was beginning to make a name for herself in the fashion industry.

Lily heard her doorbell ring. She opened the door to find a deliveryman from the local florist holding a beautiful bouquet of red roses. She couldn't imagine who would be sending her flowers and opened the attached card.

Dear Lily, These roses pale in comparison to your beauty. Peter.

His words amused Lily, and she guessed someone else wrote the card for him. She hadn't seen Peter since that day on the beach last week and questioned his motives and how he had discovered where she lived. Already late for work, she placed the flowers on the table and left the apartment for the day.

Peter had spotted Lily coming out of the boutique one evening. He secretly followed her to her apartment. Knowing where she lived would make it easier for him to pursue her. He blew a whole day's pay on those silly flowers but considered it a small price to pay if it helped persuade Lily that he had changed. If he played his cards right, his life was about to get a whole lot better.

Chapter Nineteen

Charleston, SC – 1989

CHASE AND LANEY FINISHED breakfast and discussed their plans for the day.

"Dad and I will be baling the rest of the hay. I'll be back around noon, and we can have lunch together."

"Okay. I have a few calls to make. I'm going to call Deidre to see if we can meet again."

Laney cleaned up the breakfast dishes and made her calls.

"Hi, Laney," Deidre answered. "I'm free later this week if you want to get together. We could meet at Waterfront Park. How about Friday afternoon?"

"Sounds perfect. I'll meet you at about three o'clock."

Laney went upstairs to finish cleaning out the attic. She stopped to get a sweater from her bedroom closet and couldn't help picking up the diary again. *I'll read a few pages first and then start working.*

Chase and his dad worked side by side all morning loading the hay bales on the flatbed. Chase ran the tractor while his dad guided the massive bundles into place.

"It's noon already, and we're about halfway done, son. Let's take a break and finish the rest after lunch," said Joe.

"Okay. I told Laney I'd have lunch with her, but I won't be long. Promise me you won't load those bales until I return to help you."

"We need to load it all today to bring it to the Exchange in the morning." Joe looked toward the western sky. "It's cloudy, and the wind is starting to pick up. If it rains, we might not make the deadline."

"Don't worry, Dad, we'll get it done. We'll have plenty of time this afternoon."

Chase knew how impatient his dad could be and hurried home for a quick bite to eat. Laney wasn't in the kitchen, so he assumed she might be working in the attic. He found her upstairs in the bedroom, engrossed in the diary.

"Hey, Lane, it's lunchtime."

"Oh dear, already? I started reading the diary after breakfast, and the hours flew by."

Her preoccupation with Ivy's diary was starting to annoy Chase. "I promised my dad I'd be back soon, so I don't have much time. I'll grab a sandwich."

Laney felt guilty for wasting the entire morning. "I'm sorry. I'll make it for you."

"That's okay, I can make it. By the way, we got a letter from the bank saying they didn't receive the copy of our marriage license to update your name on our account."

"I forgot to drop it off, but I promise I'll go tomorrow."

"You said that last week."

"I said I'll do it. Is it a problem, Chase?"

"All you do is bury your head in that diary. You're more concerned with what happened thirty years ago than what's going on now. You even forgot about planning our honeymoon."

"You don't understand how important this is to me. You have both your parents; you know all about them and your family history. There are no sinister secrets in your past like there appear to be in mine."

"I do understand, Laney, honestly. I would want to know the truth, too, but we still have to live our lives and take care of things around here."

"Are you saying I don't do anything?"

"No, that's not what I'm saying at all. It's just that we both have responsibilities." Chase regretted opening a can of worms, especially when he needed to return to work. "Forget I said anything."

Laney didn't appreciate Chase's accusations and lack of understanding. "I'm going for a walk," she announced as she stormed out of the back door with Rascal right behind her.

"Lane, please don't go away mad," he begged her. But Laney was already on her way to the pond with no intention of turning around.

Chase thought about going after her, but decided to give her time to think things through. After hastily eating a sandwich, he went back to his parents' house to finish loading the hay.

"Dad, I'm back," he said, assuming his father was still inside eating lunch. "Sorry I took so long. Laney and I had our first fight." When he didn't answer, Chase went outside to find him. Turning his head toward the field, Chase heard the tractor running, but his dad wasn't in the seat. *Something's wrong.*

Chase ran toward the tractor and found his dad lying on the ground with his leg pinned underneath a large bale of hay that had fallen off the fork. He rushed to his dad's side, calling out, but he didn't respond.

Chase tried to rouse his dad. "Dad, can you hear me?"

Chase couldn't budge the thousand-pound hay bale by himself, but he had to get it off his dad. He found a pair of wire cutters in the cab of the tractor and cut through the heavy wire to release the hay. As it began to break free, Chase acted quickly to push the loosened hay off his father. With the pressure relieved from his chest, Joe started to come around.

A quick observation of his contorted body told Chase that his dad had sustained several injuries. Careful not to move him, he asked, "Dad, how badly are you hurt? Can you tell if anything is broken?"

"Son? What happened?" asked Joe as he tried to clear his blurred vision.

"The hay bale fell on you. We need to get you to the hospital."

"I'll be okay," he said, trying to sit up. But when he lifted his head off the ground, he fell backward, grimacing in pain.

"Don't try to move. I'm gonna run to the house and call the ambulance. I'll be right back."

"I'm not going anywhere," said Joe, trying to disguise his anguish with a joke.

Earlier, Marjorie had gone shopping. She had just returned and was putting the groceries away as Chase came running into the house, obviously upset and in a hurry.

"Chase, what's wrong?"

His sentences were short and panicked. "Dad is hurt. A hay bale fell on him in the field. I'm calling for help." He picked up the phone and dialed 9-1-1.

Marjorie grabbed a first aid kit and ran out to the field. Joe was shaking and unresponsive by the time she got to him. She covered him with her jacket to help prevent him from going into shock.

"Stay with me, Joe." She held his hand and waited for what seemed like an eternity for help to arrive.

Chase waited in the driveway for the ambulance to direct them to the field. They drove across the grass to save time and promptly attended to Joe. They placed a splint on his broken leg and a backboard under him to support his neck and spine. On the count of three, they lifted Joe into the back of the ambulance. Marjorie climbed in next to him, and they sped off to the hospital. Chase followed in his father's truck.

Rascal ran to keep up with Laney as she walked to the pond. She was so angry at Chase for criticizing her about reading her grandmother's diary, but more so, hated the fact that they had quarreled. He only wanted to protect her from being hurt by the secrets of the past, but she needed to uncover the truth, no matter how painful it might be. Learning that her father was a scoundrel who treated her mother poorly was a devastating discovery, but it made her realize how fortunate she was to have a man like Chase as her husband.

Admittedly, she had been breaking promises and losing track of time lately. She had to strike a balance between her new life as a married woman and her quest to uncover links to her past.

"Come on, Rascal. I've got some apologizing to do."

Laney went home to wait for Chase to come home from work. She'd have his favorite meal, meatloaf and mashed potatoes, on the table when he arrived.

Chase and Marjorie sat in the waiting room while Joe went into surgery. An hour later, the doctor came out to give an update on his condition.

"Mrs. Buchanan, your husband is a lucky man. He sustained a concussion, a fractured clavicle, broken ribs, and his left leg was broken in three places. We were able to repair the breaks and reset his leg. None of the injuries are life-threatening, but he'll be laid up for several weeks to allow time to fully recover. Your son's quick actions may have saved his life."

Marjorie breathed a sigh of relief. "Thank you, doctor. When can we see him?"

"He'll be in recovery for a while, but I'll have the nurse let you know when he's awake."

"That's good news, Mom. He'll be okay," Chase consoled his mother, knowing she was putting on a brave face but was dreadfully worried about her husband on the inside.

"Oh, Chase, when I saw him lying on the ground..." She stopped herself from continuing.

"Shhh. Everything's gonna be fine. We'll take care of him when he gets home."

"Thanks, Chase. I'm sure you and Laney were just as worried as me. Where is she, by the way?"

Suddenly, Chase realized he'd forgotten to call Laney. Everything had happened so fast, and he'd had no time to contact her. He ran to the pay phone and dialed the house.

Laney had begun to worry when Chase didn't come home at the usual time. She called the Buchanan house, but no one answered. She waited another hour before the phone finally rang. She picked it up on the first ring. "Chase, is that you? Are you okay? Where are you? I'm beside myself with worry!"

"I'm so sorry. My father's in the hospital, and I didn't have a chance to call until now."

"Oh no. What happened?"

Chase told her about the accident, and she drove to the hospital to be with him and his mother. Joe came out of surgery soon after she arrived, still sleepy from the anesthesia, but resting comfortably. Marjorie sat beside his bed, exhausted.

"Laney dear, I'm so glad you're here," said Marjorie.

"Of course. How's he doing?"

"He's resting now, but I suspect he'll be in pain once the anesthesia wears off."

The nurse came in to check on Joe and give him his medications. She recommended that Marjorie go home and get some rest.

"She's right, Mom. Dad's going to be sleeping for a while, and he's in good hands."

"I know, but I can't bear to leave him here all alone."

The nurse reassured Marjorie that it would be okay to leave. "There's nothing you can do tonight. You can come back in the morning and stay as long as you'd like. You need to keep your strength up for when he comes home."

Marjorie didn't have the energy to put up a fight. She kissed her sleeping husband and said a silent prayer asking God to watch over him until she returned. Chase drove his mother home, and Laney followed them in her car. They offered to spend the night with Marjorie, but she refused.

"You two run along home. I'll be fine."

They respected her wishes on the condition that she would call if she needed anything.

Chase and Laney drove to their house. They walked in together in awkward silence. The tension between them was palpable. Laney couldn't stand it and spoke first.

"I'm sorry we fought, Chase. You were absolutely right; I've been neglecting things around here lately. Please forgive me."

"No, I'm the one who needs to apologize. I didn't see your point of view."

"How could you? My circumstances are unusual and not something you can relate to. I understand that."

"Tonight changed that for me. Seeing my dad lying there, not knowing if he was dead or alive, was horrific. Thoughts of losing him terrified me. I can't imagine how you felt to lose both your parents as a small child. I'm sorry I didn't understand that."

"And I'm so sorry I wasn't with you this afternoon."

"There wasn't much you could have done."

"I could've supported and consoled you. That's what a wife does for her husband, as your mom did for your dad. I'm your partner, Chase, by your side for whatever comes our way."

"Me too. I promise to help you find out what happened to your parents."

"And I won't let it consume my every waking thought or let things slide."

"That's a deal. Now, do we kiss and make up?" Chase started kissing her, but she stopped him. "What's wrong?"

"With your dad in the hospital, we may have to postpone our honeymoon a little longer, at least until he's back on his feet."

"Yeah, you're right. I can't leave right now. I'm sorry we have to delay it again."

"Not at all. Family comes first, no matter what. I plan to be married for the rest of my life, so a few more weeks won't make a difference."

"That's why I love you, Lane. You put your family's needs ahead of your own."

"You do the same thing, Chase. I guess that's why we were meant for each other."

That night in bed, his passionate kisses told her that all was forgotten. They were a team and would face life head-on, together.

Chapter Twenty

Charleston, SC – 1989

L ANEY GOT READY TO meet with Deidre for a second time. She tried to mentally prepare for whatever new information she might have to offer. It still wouldn't make it any easier to hear the cold, hard facts about her father.

"Thanks for meeting with me, Deidre. I was hoping you could shed some light on the details about the relationship between my mother and father. I don't really know what happened during the time leading up to her death. Did she realize she'd made a mistake in marrying him? Did she plan on leaving him? I'm just trying to understand what made her make certain choices."

"I can understand that, Laney. I'd want to know those things, too, if I were you."

"My grandmother loved her so much and was very upset that she married Peter. I don't believe my mother would have intentionally defied her. She must have had her reasons."

"I'll do the best I can to try to justify her motives. After high school, I reconnected with your mother. A few years had passed, and we had both matured. I called her, and she was very receptive to reconciling. When we met up, it was as if nothing had happened between us. We missed each other so much and buried the hatchet instantly. She shared how thrilled she was to be a mother and how much she loved you, but when she talked about Peter, the excitement stopped. I was so concerned about her."

"Why do you think she married him?"

"I wish I knew. They weren't compatible at all. She was going places, while he had no future. My guess is that she was dealing with a lot of self-esteem issues. She confided in me that she missed having a father and longed to be loved by a man. She had such talent but constantly doubted herself and sought approval, especially from the men in her life. I think she was afraid of being abandoned and turned to Peter, who she knew wouldn't leave her."

"That makes me so sad. My mother had so much to live for but never knew it."

"Ivy tried to encourage her, and I did all I could to show her that she had a bright and promising future. Without coming right out and saying it, I tried to tell her she could do better than Peter."

Laney lowered her gaze and stared forlornly at the ground.

"I'm sorry, Laney. I didn't mean to talk badly about your father. I'm sure this is very difficult to hear."

"It is, but we can't sugarcoat the truth."

"I think I could have helped her, but we ran out of time. I still remember the gut-wrenching feeling I had when I heard the news about the accident. She was so young."

Laney teared up while listening to the recounting of her mother's short life. It was a lot to deal with and stirred up her own memories of leaving her home to go live with Ivy.

"I was too young at the time to really grasp the gravity of the situation. My grandmother didn't talk about her very much, and I guess I just accepted my new life without her. There are times, though, especially now, when I wish she were here."

"Of course you do, Laney."

"I appreciate your meeting with me. You're one of the only people left who knew her so well. Talking with you makes her feel closer to me."

"You're welcome. I hope it helped in some way. Please call me if you need to talk again."

"Thanks. That means a lot to me."

Laney cried all the way home. She thought about how her life had been altered by one tragic event. *I can't get caught up in what might have been. My life is with Chase now, and that's all that matters.*

Joe wanted nothing more than to go home. His doctor finally released him, and Chase picked him up from the hospital.

"I sure missed your mama's home-cooked meals. That hospital food tasted terrible," he told Chase as he helped him out of the car and into the house.

"She's been cooking up a storm waiting for you to come home."

"Amen. A hospital is no place to get better. I need good food, my own bed to sleep in, and fresh air to breathe."

"Remember what the doctor said, Dad, you have to take it slowly and do your physical therapy until you're back to one hundred percent. It's gonna take a little time."

"I know, but I don't want to put everything on your shoulders, son. It takes a lot to keep this operation going."

"We'll be fine. If I need help, we can hire someone part-time to give me a hand. Let's wait and see how it goes."

"You're a good son, Chase. I couldn't ask for more."

Joe worked hard to regain the strength in his leg, although he still needed a walker for support. Pleased with his progress, the physical therapist predicted Joe would be walking independently by Thanksgiving. Chase and Laney took this news as their cue to take their long-overdue honeymoon.

Chase and Laney leisurely strolled along the white sandy shores of Maui. Their hotel in Ka'anapali had a spectacular view overlooking the ocean. At night, they listened to the shushing sound of the palm trees swaying outside their open balcony door. They meandered through the gift shops and boutiques in Lahaina and attended a luau complete with a roasted pig dinner and hula dancers for entertainment.

They spent the afternoons relaxing in lounge chairs and forgetting that time existed. They took snorkeling lessons and swam in the crystal-clear blue water alongside huge sea turtles. At dusk, they stopped whatever they were doing to revel in the breathtaking sunset as the huge fireball in the sky seemingly disappeared into the water.

Laney wore a plumeria flower behind her left ear, signifying her status as a married woman. Chase thought she never looked lovelier and fell more deeply in love with her. They made love nearly every day of their two-week trip and, although it didn't seem possible, grew closer to each other than ever before.

On the last day of their trip, Chase surprised Laney with a beautiful gold necklace with five plumeria flowers, each with a diamond stud in the center. He told Laney the significance of the flower.

"In Hawaiian culture, the plumeria symbolizes everything that is positive and balanced in life. That's how I feel about you and me. I love you, Mrs. Buchanan."

"I love you too, Mr. Buchanan."

The long flight back home gave them time to talk about the new memories they'd made in Hawaii and discuss their plans after returning to Charleston.

"Now that the house renovations are done and Dad is getting back on his feet, I should have time to help you find out more about your parents."

"I'd like that, Chase. Do you think we can meet with your Uncle Billy?"

"I think we can arrange that."

"That would be wonderful. I have a little more reading to do first. Before leaving for Hawaii, I reached the part when my parents got back together." Laney had a worried look on her face.

"What's wrong?"

"I'm afraid I'm getting close to details about my parents that might be difficult to read."

"I feared the diary might be disturbing at some point. I don't want to see you getting worked up or hurt."

"I admit, some sections are painful, but it's the only way I'll truly understand what happened. Ivy wrote her intimate feelings, no matter how hard it was for her to put them on paper. I owe it to my mother's memory to learn about her life."

"I understand," Chase assured her. "You know you can lean on me if things get too intense."

"Thanks. I appreciate that."

Chapter Twenty-One

Charleston, SC – 1962

PETER CONTINUED TO COURT Lily. While her success earned good money, Ivy Westfield's bank account was the ultimate goal. He would win Lily over first, then work his way into her mother's good graces. If he married Lily, her inheritance would be his too one day, and his days working on the dock would be over.

Peter took Lily out to dinner and to the movies a few times. Laney was excited to see the new musical *The Music Man* with Robert Preston and Shirley Jones. Even though he hated the movie, he kept his opinion of it to himself. He was determined to show Lily that he was polite, considerate and a perfect gentleman. He opened doors for her and pulled out her chair at the restaurant. When her leaky faucet needed to be repaired, he fixed it for her without being asked. She fell for his charade, and his time and money started paying off. But Peter knew he wouldn't stand a chance of getting close to her unless they were married. He remembered their chaste dating in high school and her strong conviction to remain pure. She didn't believe in intimacy with a man before marriage, then or now.

October 30, 1962

Dear Diary,

Today Lily told me she's seeing Peter Armstrong again. He showed up in Charleston and started courting her. I never liked that man and trust him even less. Lily is successful and happy and doesn't need the likes of him hanging around. I hope she doesn't do anything reckless.

I made my first significant purchase in years, a new Zenith color TV. The depression taught me to save every penny, but I thought it would be okay to splurge this one time. I enjoy the Ed Sullivan show on Sunday evenings and The Lucy Show. It's very different watching the news on television instead of hearing it on the radio like I used to. The news reports of the rising conflict in Vietnam are reminiscent of those from World War II. I hope our country doesn't become involved in a war again.

Lily liked the companionship and became used to having Peter around. She began to see him in a new light, much differently than the boy in high school. He was handsome and considerate and treated her right. After years of not having a male figure in her life, she appreciated a man around the house. *Am I falling for him?*

Peter trudged off to work week after week. He hated every minute of it until one day, he learned a valuable piece of information.

"Hey, Petey, when you gonna marry that pretty little girl and become a daddy?" asked one of his fellow dock workers.

"That's none of your darn business," Peter fired back.

"Well, if you ain't gonna do it, I will. Nobody is sending me to Vietnam to fight in a war."

"What are you talking about?"

"Ain't you heard? President Kennedy's got this new thing called a hardship deferment. If you got a kid, you get out of the draft. I'm gonna be one of those 'Kennedy fathers' and keep my hide out of that godforsaken country."

That night, Peter bought a copy of the *Evening Post* explaining the specifics of the deferment order. This changed things for Peter, and he stepped up his efforts with Lily. They needed to be married and pregnant right away. *Where am I gonna find enough money to buy an engagement ring?*

Lily asked Peter to come for dinner, and he eagerly accepted her invitation. He shaved and showered, and put on his best shirt and trousers. They were the only nice clothes he owned, but hopefully, all that would change soon. He arrived at Lily's door with flowers in hand.

"Thank you, Peter. These are lovely, but you shouldn't be spending so much money on me."

"You're worth it, sweetheart."

They enjoyed their dinner and talked mostly about Lily's job. She told Peter she expected a raise very soon. The news made his heart skip a beat, and he knew he must move fast. A woman like Lily would easily be swooped up by another man with far better prospects than he had.

"That's wonderful, Lily, congratulations," he told her. "Have you thought about your future?"

"If you mean with my job, I love what I do and can't imagine doing anything else."

"That's great, but I meant you and me."

"Us? To be honest, Peter, not really. You've only been back in town a short time, and we just started dating."

Peter feigned hurt by her words. "That may be true, Lily, but I have never stopped thinking about you," he said as he inched closer to her. "Ever since high school, you've been the only girl for me. Don't you know that I'm in love with you, Lily?"

This was the last thing Lily expected to hear. "I had no idea you felt this way."

"I do. I want us to be together, to get married and start a family."

"But Peter... I'm getting settled in my career and hadn't thought about having a husband, much less a family."

"I know this all seems sudden, but wouldn't it be better to have someone to share your life with?"

Lily stared at Peter, unsure how to respond. The room suddenly felt too small. She stepped out onto the balcony and drew in a few deep breaths. Peter followed her outside.

"Please don't be upset, Lily. Take some time to think about it. Let's talk about it tomorrow."

Peter left, hoping Lily would give serious thought to his proposal. He needed an engagement ring but spent every last cent on Lily and couldn't afford one. He remembered his roommate sporting a gold watch he inherited from his father. That should do the trick.

Lily showed up for work the next day with dark circles under both eyes. She'd barely slept, thinking over what Peter had said. He seemed to be more responsible, held a steady job, and showed genuine interest in her career and future. *But am I in love with him?* He didn't make her heart sing like the heroines she read about in romance books. Her feelings paled in comparison to the way her mother described meeting her father for the first time. Unable to think about it anymore, she immersed herself in her work and forgot about Peter's proposal for the rest of the day.

Lily worked on a new dress design and presented it to her boss. He had challenged her to shift focus to target young women between the ages of twenty-five and thirty-five. Lily studied potential buyers of this age group to learn their tastes in fabric, styles, and colors. She experimented with a few unique designs and garnered positive comments on her drawings.

Today, Lily proudly displayed her sketchbook on her boss's desk and waited for his reaction. The frown on his face and hesitancy in his voice discouraged her.

"It's not even remotely what I wanted. For one thing, the colors are too loud, and the hemline is far too short. I don't know who would buy this."

Lily tried to listen to his comments objectively but disagreed with his assessment.

"I think it's exactly what women in this age group are looking for," she said, defending her creations. "I've met with them, listened to their preferences, and shown them these sketches. They loved them!" Lily didn't notice her voice rising as she nearly shouted at her boss.

"Lily, please calm down."

She regained her composure and made another attempt to convince him that her drawings were indeed timely and fashionable, but her words fell on deaf ears.

"I'm sorry, I can't use these."

Dejected, Lily walked out of his office with her sketchbook under her arm. She had worked so hard, and he had abruptly dismissed her ideas. She left work early and went home to her apartment to be alone and sulk.

That evening, around six, Peter knocked on Lily's door. After having her designs rejected, Lily didn't want company. She opened the door slightly and told him she didn't feel well and asked him to come back another time. Peter tried to appear concerned and asked Lily what was wrong.

Reluctantly, Lily let Peter into her apartment. He could tell something had upset her and seized the opportunity to convince Lily she needed him for support.

"Tell me what happened."

While Lily began telling him about her boss dismissing her work, Peter positioned himself as close to her as possible. He interjected sympathetic comments here and there while she spoke. He stroked her hair while gently guiding her head onto his shoulder in a comforting gesture.

"It's going to be okay, Lily. Your boss will come to his senses, and even if he doesn't, I'm sure there are plenty of other shops that will want to hire you."

"Do you think so?"

"Of course I do. You're talented and can write your own ticket."

Lily liked having someone to confide in who was understanding and empathetic. "Thank you. I appreciate your confidence in me."

As Peter held Lily in his arms, she started to relax. He began kissing her, and she turned her face toward his. As their kiss deepened, Peter gathered as much self-control as he had. He'd move slowly and bide his time.

Pulling back, Peter looked into Lily's eyes and said, "Let's not get carried away. You've had a bad day, honey. Tomorrow is Saturday. Let's spend the day on the beach so you can forget about work. Would you like that?"

Touched by Peter's sensitivity and respect for her feelings, Lily accepted.

"I'd love that, Peter."

Lily interpreted the gleam in his eyes as anticipation for a fun day together. Peter tried his best to hide his utter delight in wearing down Lily's resistance.

They spent a peaceful, relaxing day on Folly Beach. Lily thought their relationship seemed to be heading in the right direction, and as they spent more time together, her feelings for him deepened. The only missing piece was her mother's acceptance of Peter. Ivy didn't come right out and say it, but Lily sensed she didn't care much for him.

In hopes of changing her mother's mind, Lily asked Ivy if she and Peter could come for Sunday dinner. It took a lot to convince Ivy to allow Peter into her home, but Lily was optimistic that she would warm up to him. She wanted her mother to see that Peter had changed and cared about her.

"Good afternoon, Mrs. Westfield," Peter said politely. "Thank you for inviting me to dinner. These are for you."

The hair on the back of Ivy's neck stood up as she accepted the flowers from Peter. "How nice of you. I'll put these in a vase," she said, suspicious about his true intentions.

The dinner conversation was sparse and awkward. Ivy asked Peter, "Tell me, what have you been doing since returning to Charleston?"

"Peter has a steady job working on the docks," said Lily, trying to portray him as responsible and reliable. "And he's very handy around the house."

"Is that so? Do you plan to stay in your job?"

"Yes, ma'am. I make a good wage and am saving my money for the future."

"Well, it's always a good plan to save for a rainy day," said Ivy, unimpressed.

After dessert, Lily and Peter said their goodbyes. "Thank you for the delicious dinner, ma'am. I sure appreciate being invited to your home."

"I'd do the same for any of Lily's friends," Ivy replied coolly.

December 4, 1962

Dear Diary,

It took every ounce of my being to hold my tongue while dining with Lily and Peter tonight. I wanted to tell Lily that she could do so much better than him. She is falling for his charm and attention, but I can see right through him. That man is up to something, and I plan to keep a close eye on him.

Peter took Lily home while hiding his distaste for Ivy. He had ignored her disparaging glares throughout dinner while trying to show how much he cared for her daughter. He made up his mind to propose to Lily again, before her mother talked her out of it. He went to the local pawn shop to find the best ring he could afford.

"Whattaya got there?"

"My dad left me this gold watch, but I'm not much for jewelry. What's it worth?"

The man behind the counter looked it over and said, "I'll give you fifty bucks for it."

"That's a solid gold watch. You know it's worth more than that." Peter looked through the jewelry case and spied a small but decent-sized diamond ring. "Tell you what... I'll trade you this watch for that engagement ring. What do you say? Is it a deal?"

The man knew he could sell the watch for a lot more than what the cheap ring was worth. "Okay, you got a deal."

With the ring in his pocket, Peter went to Lily's apartment after work, and they shared a light supper. Afterward, they moved to the sofa, and Peter started his marriage campaign.

"Did you read the latest news about Vietnam?"

"No. Are things getting worse? Do you think we'll be involved soon?"

"I'm not sure. The United States has already started sending troops over there. It may only be a matter of time until men are drafted again."

"Oh no! I didn't realize that. I don't want that to happen to you or any of the men our age."

"Me neither. I would hate the thought of leaving you and Charleston."

"I heard they don't take married men or fathers. Is that true?"

"Yes, that's true." The time had come for Peter to make his move.

"I love you, Lily," he told her in a deep, throaty voice. "Tell me you love me too."

"Oh, Peter," she said between his kisses, not yet ready to declare love for him.

Peter stopped kissing her and dropped to one knee. "I care about you, Lily, more than anyone I've ever known. You know we're right for each other. Marry me." He opened the ring box and put the gold band with a small diamond chip on her finger. "Say yes, honey."

Lily tried to rationalize his proposal in her mind. She wasn't madly in love with him but thought perhaps she would come to love him in time. She recalled the difficult time Ivy had living alone after her husband died. Lily didn't want to live a lonely life with nothing but her career, but wasn't sure she was ready to make such a life-changing commitment.

"Please give me some time to think about it. I wouldn't feel right accepting without having my mother's blessing."

"Of course. But don't wait too long. I want to be your husband and make you Mrs. Peter Armstrong as soon as possible."

Lily promised to give him an answer within the next day or so. She attempted to calm the flurry of thoughts running through her mind as she considered both the pros and cons of marriage. Peter waited with bated breath for her decision.

Chapter Twenty-Two

Charleston, SC – 1962

THE NEXT MORNING, LILY reached for the pink Princess telephone on her bedside table and dialed her mother's number.

"Hello, Mother. I have the afternoon off. Would you like to meet for lunch today?"

"Oh, Lily dear," Ivy said warmly. "I'd love to. Where would you like to go?"

"How about the Tea Room? That's always been a favorite of ours."

"Perfect. I'll make the reservations for noon."

The Victorian Tea Room served a delicious assortment of finger sandwiches, delicate pastries, and exotic teas on exquisite fine china. Ivy arrived first.

"Hello. I have a reservation for two for Ivy Westfield."

"Of course, Mrs. Westfield. Please follow me."

The hostess led Ivy to a small, intimate dining room decorated in nineteenth-century décor with ornate, velvet furnishings. The papered walls were dotted with shelves displaying interesting knick-knacks. Lily breezed through the door a few minutes later and spotted Ivy. She kissed her mother on the cheek and sat down at the table. They took a few minutes to make their selections, and Ivy gestured to the waitress to take their order.

"This is an unexpected treat. We don't get together like this often enough, Lily."

"I'm sorry, Mother. I've been so busy with work. Time seems to be at a premium lately."

"Anything else keeping you busy, dear?" Ivy didn't come right out and mention Peter, but Lily knew what she was hinting at.

"Yes. Peter and I have been seeing a lot of one another, and it's getting serious. That's what I wanted to talk about today."

"I'm listening," said Ivy, bracing herself.

"I'll come right out and say it, Mother. Peter asked me to marry him, and I think I'm going to accept."

"Oh Lily, why would you want to marry him? You've only been dating a short time, and his track record isn't the best."

"That's true, but he's changed. He's made great strides in improving himself and longs for a nice life with a wife and family."

"I bet he does." The words were out of Ivy's mouth before she could stop them.

"What does that mean?"

"You're a successful young woman with means, which is rare in this day and age. How can you be sure he's interested in you and not in your checkbook?"

Ivy's insinuation of Peter's motives angered Lily. "Mother! That's a horrible thing to say!"

"I'm sorry, dear, but I have good cause to think this way. Peter spent time in jail as a teenager and has no formal education. You don't have much experience dating men, and I don't want to see you fall for the first one who shows you attention."

"You don't understand me, Mother, you never have!"

"I understand more than you think. Your father died when you were a baby, and you've always dreamed of having a traditional family. I raised you myself, without a husband. It's understandable that you want more than that for yourself, but I don't think Peter is the right man to give you what you want."

"I'm not you, Mother. I don't need the support of a husband. Obviously, I can live alone, I just prefer not to. Peter and I enjoy being together."

"Spending time together and being married with a family are two different things."

Lily's frustration mounted. Ivy had made up her mind about Peter, and nothing she could say would change that. It reminded Lily of her high school days and their tumultuous arguments.

"I'm sorry we can't agree on this, Mother. I've decided to accept Peter's proposal and would like your blessing."

Ivy was torn. Lily marrying Peter was a mistake, but if she refused to accept it, she'd risk losing her. If she agreed with Lily's decision, Ivy would keep a close eye on Peter and make sure he didn't step out of line.

"I love you, Lily, and only want what's best for you. If you believe in your heart that marrying Peter is what you want, I won't protest."

"Does that mean we have your blessing?"

Ivy hesitated before answering. "Yes," she said quietly. "I wish you all the happiness you deserve."

"Thank you, Mother. This means the world to me, and I'm sure Peter will be happy too!"

"You're welcome, dear. Let me know how I can help with the wedding."

"You don't have to worry about that, Mother. I don't want anything elaborate."

"As you wish." Although Ivy didn't want to miss the privilege of being the mother of the bride, she was grateful she wouldn't have to put on the pretense in front of a large gathering that she approved of their union.

January 13, 1963

Dear Diary,

My heart is heavy. Lily and Peter plan to marry, and I think she's making a big mistake. I don't want her to be hurt, but I cannot stop her. All I can do is be there for her when she needs me.

These times are scary, and it's so hard to shoulder all my responsibilities alone. There may be another war starting soon, and many of the young men who help me with the chores and gardens might be drafted. Preston helps when he can, but he has his own life to live. I wish my Hank were here to help me.

When Lily told Peter she accepted his proposal, he wasted no time putting the wheels in motion. He arranged for the justice of the peace to perform the ceremony, and they went to City Hall for the license.

"You've made me so happy, Lily. Soon we'll be husband and wife. When should I start moving my things into the apartment?"

"Whoa, Peter, slow down. Let me catch my breath. We just got engaged."

"It's just that I love you so much and want to start our life together as soon as possible."

Flattered by his urgency to wed, Lily replied, "Me too. I guess we can start clearing some room for your things."

A week later, Lily and Peter were married in an austere City Hall office on Broad Street in Charleston. Lily wore a simple white dress and a single gardenia in her hair. Ivy attended and served as a witness with one of the secretaries acting as the second. No one attended on Peter's side. Afterward, Ivy treated the two of them to lunch. She snapped a wedding photo of them with her Brownie camera, the only memento of the day.

Laney found the photo she kept of her parents' wedding and looked at it through a different lens this time. She studied her mother's expression, looking closely for a hint of how she may have felt on her wedding day. Her smile looked forced, not radiant like Ivy's or Laney's wedding portraits. Her father's body wasn't close to her mother's, as you would expect with newlyweds. It saddened Laney to think of her mother marrying for convenience. She hoped her birth would bring joy and happiness to Lily, even if only for a short time. She read on.

Peter moved in on the same day they were married. The small one-bedroom apartment was ample for Lily, and she tried to make it work for two people. Not surprisingly, Peter had no furniture of his own and very few possessions.

"I cleared the drawers on the left side of the dresser and half the closet for you," Lily told Peter.

"Thanks. It's more than enough room."

Their first night together was awkward. Lily had never slept with a man before and didn't really know what to expect. To his credit, Peter took his time making love to her.

"I love you, Lily, and I've waited a long time for this night."

"I love you too, Peter. Please be gentle." Lily closed her eyes.

The next morning, Lily struggled with many different emotions. She had never experienced intimacy with a man before. She thought there would be more tender moments and caresses. They didn't cuddle together afterward or whisper words of love everlasting. *Is this what true love feels like? Will we grow closer to each other?*

Each day, Peter and Lily ate breakfast together, went to work in the morning, and returned home about the same time in the evening. Peter helped with the cooking and housekeeping, even though he hated performing household chores. It wasn't until the trash bin overflowed that he would take it upon himself to empty it, or the supply of towels depleted, before he would offer to help with the laundry.

After a month of married life, Peter realized giving up his bachelor status came with a price. Domestic life may have suited others, but he'd rather be at the bar after work, drinking with his buddies, than washing dishes. He reminded himself that the sacrifice was relatively small compared to the windfall he expected and the chance to avoid the draft. With a little luck and timing, the deferment would be in the bag.

Lily left work early one Friday. She had an upset stomach and thought maybe the chicken salad she had eaten for lunch hadn't agreed with her. She drank a glass of seltzer water, but it did nothing to calm her queasiness. She went to bed early, hoping to sleep it off, but woke up the next morning feeling much worse. After a mad dash to the bathroom, she emptied the contents of her stomach and went back to bed. Thankfully, it was Saturday, and she didn't have to go to work. However, she planned to go shopping with her mother that afternoon.

Maybe I'll feel better in a little while. That didn't happen. She continued vomiting for much of the morning and called her mother at 11:30 to cancel their date.

"I'm sorry you're not feeling well. Do you want me to come over?"

"No. I think I ate something yesterday that didn't agree with me. I'm sure I'll be okay after a little rest."

"It's no bother at all," Ivy insisted. "I'll be over in about half an hour with some broth and soda crackers." Lily welcomed her mother's concern and didn't object.

When Ivy arrived, Lily had just returned to bed after another trip to the bathroom. Ivy placed a cool washcloth on her daughter's forehead and covered her with a blanket.

"Oh, Mom, I've never felt so bad. What's wrong with me?"

"Lily, dear, have you given any thought to the possibility that perhaps you're pregnant?"

"No! Do you think that's why I've been so nauseous?"

"There's a better than average chance that's the reason. You need to see your doctor to find out one way or the other."

Lily scheduled an appointment with her doctor for a blood test Monday morning. She waited all day for the results. Each time the phone rang, Lily held her breath. First, her boss called asking when she planned to return to work. Next, her mother checked in on her. The third time the phone rang, it was the doctor's office.

"Hello, Mrs. Armstrong. I have your test results. Congratulations, you and your husband are expecting." Lily froze and dropped the phone on the floor.

Peter came home from work, and Lily told him the news.

"Are you sure?"

"Yes, I'm positive. My doctor performed a blood test to confirm it."

"Lily, darling, that's wonderful news! Now we know why you were sick. What can I do to help you?"

Peter prepared soup for her and made her comfortable. Lily ate a small amount before taking a nap. Ivy called to check on her, and Peter told her she was resting. Wanting to see her daughter for herself, she decided to pay them a visit later that afternoon.

"Mother, so good to see you."

"How are you feeling, Lily?"

"I'm glad you asked... We have some news. Peter and I are expecting."

Ivy wasn't surprised, but that didn't lessen the blow. She sat back on the sofa, taking a deep breath and a minute to compose herself. With grace and dignity, she swallowed her true feelings and congratulated them both.

"Well, the arrival of a baby is a joyous event, and I'm very happy for both of you," she said as enthusiastically as possible.

"Thank you, Mother," Lily said as she hugged Ivy, clutching her tightly for both moral and emotional support.

"Yes," Peter chimed in, "Thank you for your blessing."

Ivy acknowledged his reply but turned away, trying to avoid looking him in the eyes. She feared she would reveal her true feelings about him, but knew that wouldn't help Lily. Instead, she focused on the positive.

"I'm going to be a grandmother. Now that really is good news!"

Lily planned to work as long as she could until the baby arrived. She made a makeshift nursery in the corner of their bedroom. Ivy bought all the furniture, clothes, cloth diapers, bottles, and blankets. She kept a watchful eye on her daughter for any signs that Peter may not be treating her right. She'd be ready and waiting to take Lily in if Peter got out of line.

At 2:25 p.m. on January 23, 1964, Lily delivered her baby. Peter was at work with no way to contact him. When he came home to an empty apartment, he saw the note on the kitchen table from Ivy saying Lily's labor had started and they'd gone to the hospital.

Seeing her daughter holding her newborn baby melted Ivy's heart. Exhausted from twenty hours of labor, Lily had the radiant glow of a new mother. Ivy recalled her own post-delivery pain and remembered how it disappeared the minute she gazed into the sweet and tender eyes of her baby. Lily now looked at her daughter the same way.

"Meet your granddaughter, Mother. Her name is Elaine Henrietta. We'll call her Laney for short."

"She's precious! And what a beautiful name!" Ivy was touched that Lily memorialized her father by choosing Henrietta for the baby's middle name. She held her granddaughter in her arms, and three generations of Westfield women enjoyed a quiet moment together.

The magical spell was broken when Peter entered the room holding an oversized teddy bear. As he approached Lily's bed, Ivy smelled liquor on his breath and moved away from him with the baby in her arms.

"How's my girl?" he bellowed, ignoring Ivy.

He plopped the teddy bear down on the chair and leaned over Lily to give her a kiss.

"Where have you been?"

"At work, but I came as soon as I saw the note."

Lily knew he was lying, but chose to ignore it. This wasn't the time or place.

Ivy resisted the temptation to take Lily and the baby home with her to protect them from this vile man. She excused herself and told Lily she would be back again the next day.

Without so much as a word to Peter, she handed the baby to Lily and left the room.

"What's eating her?"

"Never mind, Peter. Don't you want to meet your daughter?"

"Of course." He peeked inside the blanket to see the baby for the first time. "She looks a little like me, don't you think?"

"It's much too soon to tell."

January 23, 1964

Dear Diary,

I'm a grandmother. The newest addition to the Westfield lineage is Elaine Henrietta, named for my dear Hank. She is sweet and innocent, even if she is one-half Armstrong. I can already see that this child will have a tough row to hoe with a father such as hers. I will do my best to stay close to my dear Lily and precious granddaughter, Laney, for they are my whole world, and I love them more than anything. Dear Lord, watch over and protect my girls.

The first few weeks at home were a busy time for Lily and the baby. Lily got up every two hours to feed Laney while Peter slept soundly in their bed. In the morning, he ate his breakfast and left a sink full of dishes for Lily to tend to while he went off to work.

Ivy stopped by each afternoon to help with the baby and conveniently left before Peter came home. It became difficult to afford their apartment on Peter's salary alone, and he told Lily she needed to return to work. Ivy was all too eager to babysit Laney each day and volunteered immediately. She kept the baby at her house, and Lily picked her up each night after work.

Ivy pulled all Lily's baby things out of the attic. She set up the crib again in Lily's old room, complete with freshly washed baby blankets, bibs, and assorted clothes. Ivy adored her new granddaughter and felt blessed to have the opportunity to nurture her and watch her grow.

May 11, 1964

Dear Diary,

The house is full of love and laughter once again. Little Laney is an angel sent from heaven, and I'm blessed to have her here with me. Being a grandmother is so different from raising Lily. I enjoy the simple things, such as feeding and bathing Laney and rocking her to sleep. The sweet scent of her hair, the soft touch of her skin, and the gentle cooing sounds she makes remind me of Lily. I recall how Hank would come home from work and go straight to the nursery to spend time with her. I know he would love our little Laney girl just as much as I do. It amazes me that this tiny baby can fill my heart and ease my loneliness. Thank you, Lord, for sending her to me.

Lily somehow managed to keep her mind on her work while juggling motherhood and marriage. Peter hardly lifted a finger to help her with the baby and gradually stopped helping with household chores. He came home late in the evening, well after his job had ended. His paycheck got smaller each week, and Lily questioned whether he went to work at all. If she mentioned anything about it to him, a fight would inevitably ensue, culminating in Peter walking out and returning after two in the morning with liquor on his breath.

One Friday evening after work, Lily arrived at Ivy's house to pick up Laney. Lily seemed out of sorts. Her hair and clothes looked disheveled, she appeared tired and worn out, and her voice sounded sad.

"Lily, are you all right?"

"Just tired, Mom."

"Is it your job? Taking care of Laney? Is it Peter?" Lily couldn't answer her mother. She stared blankly ahead. Ivy stepped closer and wrapped her in a hug. "Or maybe it's all of the above."

Lily could no longer hold back her emotions and began to confide in her mother.

"Nothing is turning out the way I planned," she cried. "Peter is hardly around and in a foul mood whenever he remembers he has a wife and child at home. He's drinking a lot, and I'm not sure if he's still working."

Ivy contained her anger and let her daughter continue talking, even though her words were tearing her apart inside.

"He doesn't even acknowledge Laney, let alone help me take care of her. I'm worn out trying to manage everything and don't know what to do."

Ivy held her daughter close, trying to comfort her. She had seen this coming and felt guilty for not being more forceful in trying to talk Lily out of marrying Peter. Nevertheless, she remained calm to help Lily determine the next steps.

She needed to get Lily out of that apartment and away from Peter, but knew it would not be easy. Lily would protest, thinking it would be best for the baby to have both parents, no matter what the circumstances. Her lifelong desire to have a happy little family blinded her to Peter's ways.

"You can always come back home, Lily. You and Laney can move in anytime you like."

"I know that, Mother, but I'm determined to make this work. Maybe Peter needs time to adjust to being a husband and father."

Lily didn't believe her own words even as she spoke them aloud. However, she still wanted to give her marriage a chance.

Lily went home with Laney to a cold, dark apartment. At 7 p.m., Peter still hadn't returned from work. She put Laney in her crib and made herself a sandwich for dinner. Peter came home around nine, clearly drunk. He threw himself onto the sofa and ordered Lily to get him something to eat.

In no mood to deal with a drunken husband, she said, "Get it yourself." Lily went into the bedroom, locking the door behind her. To her relief, she heard the front door open and close, signaling Peter was gone.

At least I can get a good night's sleep. I'll deal with this tomorrow.

Peter realized Lily wouldn't tolerate his behavior for very long. After losing his job on the docks, he started working for one of his old friends collecting debts and usually ended up at the local tavern about midday. His plan to let Lily work to support him had worked out so far, but he didn't want to jeopardize the arrangement. He decided to smooth-talk Lily, show a little concern, and help out...at least for a bit.

Ivy called her brother Preston to enlist his help with Lily once again. She asked him to follow Peter to find out where he went every day. Preston agreed to help his sister and niece and discreetly started following Peter.

After a few days, he reported to Ivy that Peter spent his time hanging around with felons in town. Most afternoons, he frequented the local bar. Ivy's suspicions were confirmed; however, she didn't know what to do next. Preston recommended continuing to keep an eye on Peter.

"Eventually, he'll land himself in jail, and your troubles will be over."

"Let's hope so."

"I'll alert my friend at the sheriff's department to be on the lookout for suspicious activity."

Peter stood in a dark alley arguing with a man to pay up or face the consequences. He had the man in a chokehold when he saw the deputy sheriff's car come to a stop. The officer got out of the car and approached Peter and the man. Peter let go of his hold on him, and they both took off running. Realizing it was a close call, Peter vowed to be more careful.

While walking home, he recognized Preston Spencer standing across the street from the apartment. He surmised that Ivy had sent him to spy on his comings and goings, just like when he and Lily were in high school. Peter knew he'd better shape up.

When Lily arrived home from work, she didn't expect Peter to be home. He had emptied the trash, washed all the dishes in the sink, and had dinner on the table.

"What's all this?"

"It's the least I can do, Lily," he told her with a faint hint of sincerity in his voice. "You've been working so hard and deserve a break."

Lily didn't buy this abrupt change in Peter and asked him, "Why all of a sudden are you realizing this?"

Peter apologized for his deplorable behavior. He told Lily his new responsibilities overwhelmed him. He further explained that his fractured relationship with his father left him ill-equipped to be a good husband and dad.

"I was scared, Lily. Please forgive me," he pleaded.

Once again, Lily found herself struggling with her inner voices: one saying throw him out and the other saying to give him another chance. The second voice won, and she decided to let Peter prove himself, but not before she got a few things straightened out.

"I believe you, Peter, but I want to know where you go every day. Have you lost your job?"

"Yes, but I found another one right away, working for an old friend. I didn't want to worry you with all you have going on, so I didn't say anything about it."

"What about the drinking? You've been coming home drunk on a regular basis. It's not good for Laney or me to have you soused all the time."

Peter promised to quit drinking, blaming that, too, on his insecurity about being a parent and spouse. "Please, Lily, let me show you that I can be the husband you want me to be."

Lily agreed but promised herself to wait and see what happened before believing that Peter had miraculously changed.

With Lily, Ivy, and Preston all keeping a watchful eye on Peter, he got on the straight-and-narrow path. He got his job back, and laid off the liquor. He came home each night and helped Lily with the baby. For a moment, he thought maybe domestic life wasn't so bad after all. Laney was a good baby and worked her way into his heart. He tried his best to maintain this new lifestyle, but old habits die hard.

Chapter Twenty-Three

Charleston, SC – 1989

LANEY HAD TO PUT down the diary and walk away from it for a while. Her father was much worse than she'd ever thought. Ivy had kept her opinions about Peter to herself to spare Laney's feelings. She understood her grandmother's intentions were based purely on her love for her.

Reading about the early months of her mother's marriage filled Laney with a quiet sadness. By contrast, she and Chase had been practically inseparable since returning from their honeymoon. Chase worked just next door on his father's farm while Laney kept busy with household chores, shopping, and helping her new mother-in-law with canning and other small tasks. Marjorie shared handwritten recipe cards for Laney to add to her growing collection and introduced her to the women in her church group. Together they volunteered for various causes, helping members of their community whenever they could. The life she and Chase were building felt simple and true, filled with family, shared work, and a love that lightened every burden.

"Laney, you remind me so much of Ivy," commented Marjorie one afternoon. "She never hesitated to help her friends and neighbors in need."

"Thanks, Mom, that's the highest compliment I could ever receive."

It felt completely natural to call her mother-in-law "mom" now. They had always been close, but since her marriage to Chase, their relationship had grown deeper. It felt good to be loved and embraced by Marjorie and have a mother to dote on her, and likewise with Chase's dad. He had all the qualities and characteristics of the father she always dreamed of having.

"I've been thinking a lot about my grandmother lately. It must have been so hard for her to lose both her husband and her daughter so tragically."

"I agree. But she found great comfort in raising you and watching you grow into a successful young woman. She was so proud of you and often talked about your accomplishments in New York."

Laney appreciated knowing that Ivy found pride and solace in her only granddaughter. Without Ivy, Lord only knows how her life would have turned out.

"I guess you know all about the letter she wrote and the mystery surrounding my parents' death."

"Yes, Chase filled us in. Is there anything I can do to help?"

"I would like to visit Chase's Uncle Billy. He knew my Uncle Preston and my father and might have some information. Would you come with us, for moral support?"

"Of course I will," Marjorie replied.

"Thanks so much. I would like that."

After the dinner dishes had been washed and put away, Laney asked Chase if he had arranged the meeting with Uncle Billy.

"Yes, they said we could come any weekday after one o'clock. It's after lunch and early enough in the day that he's not too tired." Once again, he cautioned her not to get her hopes up, only to be disappointed if Uncle Billy's memory failed him.

"I promise I won't, Chase. I understand it's a long shot, but it's the only one I have right now."

"I know, sweetheart. I just don't want to see you disappointed."

Now, more than ever, she wanted to hear all the details, no matter how painful they may be. Knowing the full truth about her father would quell any misconceptions she still held on to, thus allowing Laney to move on with her life.

Chase wasn't worried as much about his great uncle not remembering the incident as he was about him revealing details that would be too distressing for Laney to hear. He admired her courage but wanted to protect her. Despite the agony over learning about her mother's pain and suffering, Laney kept returning to the diary.

Charleston, SC – 1968

March 20, 1968

Dear Diary,

Caring for a child at my age is a little more daunting than I anticipated, hence the long lapse in my entries. Laney remains the apple of my eye. She is so full of life, and each day is an adventure with her. She loves to be outdoors and enjoys helping in the garden and our little trips to the beach.

Spring has arrived, and it's time to prepare the soil for planting. The Vietnam War has taken many of our regular workers, but soon Herb Martin will be returning from Florida to help, just as he has done for the past twelve years. I think we will add some cabbage and okra this year.

Lily's optimism that her marriage could work was short-lived. Peter started drinking again, spending most of what he earned at the bar. Lily sensed he was getting bored and wanted out of the marriage. Things were getting out of control, and she, too, was ready to call it quits. Her fantasies of the perfect life and family were a pipe dream that she needed to let go of.

The final straw came when she and Peter got into another fight, the worst one yet. He started screaming at her for no reason about the dinner she put on the table. He didn't like the way she had prepared the green beans, picked up the dish, and threw it across the room. Laney squirmed in her chair next to Peter and began to cry. Her wailing incited him further, and next, he picked up a glass and hurled it against the wall just over Lily's head. Shards of glass went sailing through the air, and she covered Laney's head to protect her.

"No more," she screamed. "I will not have you hurting my baby. Get out!"

Peter yelled back at her, "With pleasure. Who needs you and that little brat anyway?"

She scooped the child into her arms and ran into the bedroom, locking the door behind them. A few minutes later, she heard the front door close, signifying Peter had gone and they could safely come out.

Peter headed to his favorite bar to drink away his troubles.

"Well, if it isn't old Petey Armstrong," said the bartender. "Where have you been hiding yourself? The wife keeping you on a short leash?"

Peter was already in a foul mood and not about to take any ribbing. He fired back, "What business is it of yours? And another thing, I couldn't care less about my wife. She doesn't run my life." He slammed his fist on the bar and demanded a beer.

"Hey now, calm down. No need to get all riled up."

Peter disdained the role of dutiful husband and hated being a father even more. He felt that Lily and Laney were a noose around his neck and wanted out. The longer he sat at the bar, the worse his disposition became, and he headed home to have it out with Lily.

Lily put Laney to bed and soaked in a soothing, hot bubble bath, trying to relax and shed the tension of the fight. She had no idea if or when Peter would show up.

When Peter finally did come home a little after ten, he had fire in his eyes. Lily braced herself for another confrontation. She could endure the usual shouting match but wouldn't put up with any physical violence, especially where Laney was concerned. Peter started his tirade.

"Look at you all cleaned up and pretty. Expecting someone, Lily?"

"What on earth are you talking about, Peter? I just took a bath to unwind." she asked. Certainly, he didn't think she had the time or desire for another man.

"You don't get all cleaned up like that for me. Who is it you're waiting for, Lily...your boss maybe?"

Lily wouldn't stand for this ridiculous accusation and contemplated leaving with Laney when Peter passed out on the couch. For a split second, she hoped he was dead. She locked herself and Laney in her room for the night and prayed for an end to this life of misery. But for now, she'd have to keep trudging along until she could make plans to leave.

Lily's new project at work demanded she work late hours to meet a deadline. Knowing she'd be home late on Friday, she arranged for Laney to sleep at Ivy's house overnight, which thrilled the child. Laney adored her grandmother. Sometimes she felt that Laney would rather be at Ivy's house than her own home...not that she blamed her.

Lily finished working after seven p.m. Since they only had one car, she usually took the bus home, but the last one stopped running at six. She tried calling Peter to come and pick her up, but she couldn't reach him. She had no choice but to spend the money on a cab.

She arrived home to an empty apartment. Assuming Peter was out drinking again, Lily ate a light supper alone and went to bed. Some time after midnight she heard him stumble through the door, his heavy footsteps echoing down the hallway. The next morning, Lily called Ivy to let her know she would be picking up Laney after lunch.

Peter didn't wake until nearly noon. When he finally stirred, he shuffled into the bathroom to shower and shave.

"It's about time you got up," Lily said, unable to keep the edge from her voice.

Peter squinted against the daylight streaming through the window. "It's my day off. Besides, I don't have plans until later."

"What plans? I need the car to pick up Laney from my mother's today."

"I'm meeting a guy from work," he said. "We're going to the marina to look at a boat he wants to fix up."

"Fine. Then let me drop you there," Lily snapped. "I'll take the car and get Laney."

Peter stared at her. "And how exactly am I supposed to get home?"

"The same way I did last night," she shot back. "Take a cab."

Neither of them spoke as Peter slid behind the wheel and started the car. The silence was thick—but it didn't last.

"Laney and I might stay at my mother's tonight," Lily muttered.

"That suits me fine," Peter fired back, gripping the steering wheel more tightly. "You can move in with her for all I care."

"I knew you never cared about me, Peter." Her voice dropped, heavier now that she finally allowed herself to believe it.

The argument escalated as they drove, voices rising and tension tightening with every mile. The narrow road curved along a steep embankment, but Peter's attention stayed fixed on Lily.

At the height of the argument, his grip faltered. The car drifted.

"Peter!" Lily screamed, grabbing for the steering wheel.

He shoved her away and jerked the car back toward the road. For a split second, his eyes flicked to her—

"Look out!" Lily shouted.

He turned back. A man stood in the road.

The impact came with a sickening thud.

The car lurched, tires losing grip as it veered off the shoulder. It careened over the embankment, metal shrieking against rock as it tumbled—once, twice—before slamming to a brutal stop.

Silence.

Then Peter groaned.

Blood trickled down the side of his face, but he was conscious.

He turned slowly.

"Lily?"

Her head was slumped against the window, unmoving.

A thin curl of smoke drifted from the front of the car. Flames flickered beneath the hood, the sharp stench of burning fuel filling the air.

"Lily, wake up!" He reached for her, but she didn't respond.

The fire spread quickly.

Peter lunged for the door. It wouldn't budge. He slammed his shoulder against it—once, twice—nothing. Desperate, he cranked the window down and forced himself through, scraping his arms as he tumbled onto the ground. He staggered to his feet and rushed to the passenger side, but he was too late.

Flames surged, forcing him back. Heat blasted against his skin as he stumbled into the brush. He could only watch.

Lily never moved. Never knew what happened.

Shaking, Peter tore the sleeve from his shirt and pressed it to his bleeding head as he backed away from the wreck. Then he turned and clawed his way up the embankment.

At the top, he froze.

The man lay crumpled in the grass, his body twisted at an unnatural angle. He was dead.

Peter's pulse pounded in his ears. His thoughts spiraled.

Preston. The police. They were already closing in. A double homicide would be enough to lock him up for good.

He looked back at the burning wreck below.

And then the thought came. Sudden. Clear. Impossible to ignore.

If they found the car... if they found two bodies inside... no one would question it.

No one would look for him.

The realization settled over him, cold and certain.

With trembling hands, Peter turned back to the dead man. Grabbing him beneath the shoulders, he began to drag the body toward the embankment. The weight was heavy and unyielding, the ground scraping against the man's back as Peter slipped on the loose gravel.

By the time he reached the wreck, the fire had begun to die down, leaving a smoldering shell.

Peter wrapped what remained of his shirt around his hands and reached for the driver's door.

With a strained grunt, he forced it open.

He hauled the body upright and shoved it behind the wheel. The man's head slumped forward against the dashboard.

For a moment, Peter hesitated.

His eyes shifted to the passenger seat. To Lily. The sight of her—still, lifeless—hit him all at once. He turned away and vomited, his body convulsing. When it passed, he wiped his mouth and forced himself to move.

Reaching into his pocket, he pulled out his wallet and tossed it beside the wreck. Inside was everything the authorities would need—his driver's license, his name, the life he was about to abandon.

Peter took one last look, then he turned and ran.

Branches clawed at his arms as he disappeared into the woods, stumbling over roots and stones, driven by a single instinct—to get as far away as possible.

Ivy and Laney drove home from the movies late that morning, Laney excitedly babbling about how much fun she had. They'd had a wonderful weekend together, and Ivy found herself wishing that Laney could stay with her all the time. As she was making lunch and waiting for Lily to pick her up, Ivy wondered why Lily hadn't arrived yet. By three o'clock, she tried calling Lily's apartment, but no one answered.

"Is my mommy coming soon?"

"She must be on her way," Ivy told her granddaughter. "Here, I'll put the television on for you while we wait." She walked to the television and turned the dial until she found *The Bugs Bunny Show.*

After two more hours passed, with no sign of Lily, Ivy began to worry in earnest. She called Lily's apartment again, but there was still no answer. Finally, she called her brother, Preston, and explained the situation, and he offered to go look for her. He decided to start at Lily's apartment and work his way back toward Ivy's house.

As he was pulling out of his driveway the sheriff's car rolled in behind him, blocking the road.

"I'm in a hurry, Mike," Preston called through the open window. "Can you let me pass?"

Sheriff Mike Dawson didn't move the vehicle. Instead, he stepped out of his car and slowly removed his hat, turning it in his hands as he lowered his gaze.

A flicker of unease passed through Preston.

"Something wrong, Mike?"

The sheriff hesitated before speaking.

Gathering his courage, the sheriff told Preston, "I've got some bad news."

Preston didn't immediately make the connection that the "bad news" could be tied to the reason Ivy couldn't locate Lily.

"Out with it... I'm on my way to find Lily," he said, annoyed that Mike was dawdling when he was in such a hurry.

The sheriff hesitated again, then rested a hand on Preston's shoulder.

"Preston... I'm afraid there's been an accident involving Lily and Peter. Neither of them survived. I'm so sorry, Preston."

Preston ran his hand through his hair. He was shocked by the news but, more importantly, worried about how to tell Ivy that her daughter and son-in-law were both dead.

"Are you sure, Mike?"

"Yes, I'm sure. It was Peter's car, and they were both still in it." Mike hated being the bearer of such tragic news. All he could do was repeat, "I'm so sorry, Preston."

"Thanks, Mike. Can you give me a lift to my sister's house?" he asked, too shaken to drive.

"Sure thing. I'll radio the coroner's office to pick up the bodies."

In town at a local drinking establishment, the bartender called out, "Hey, Chuck, the sheriff's on the phone for you."

Chuck Morgan finished the last sip of his beer and answered the call. After returning the phone to its cradle, he said,

"Coroner duty calls," as he laid down some money on the bar to settle his tab.

Chuck had had a few too many beers that night. He arrived at the scene of the crash a little tipsy and tired. The smell of burning bodies made him vomit. He put them in body bags and loaded them into his truck. He picked up a wallet lying on the ground a few feet away from the wreckage. It was after midnight when he returned to the morgue to complete the report.

"I'm getting too old for this," remarked Chuck as he filled out the paperwork. One female, Lillian Armstrong. One male, Peter Armstrong. Cause of death: burns, smoke inhalation.

When Ivy saw the sheriff's car pull into the driveway, she ran to the front door. Laney had fallen asleep on the sofa after waiting so long for her mother to come for her. Ivy walked outside slowly and stood at the top of the porch steps. An eerie feeling overcame her, similar to when the Western Union man delivered the telegram about Hank's death in the war. She wrapped her sweater tightly around herself and braced for whatever they came to tell her.

Preston reached her first. He climbed the steps and encircled Ivy in his arms. Preston wasn't naturally an affectionate person, so she knew the news must be bad.

"What is it, Preston? Tell me, please!"

"It's Lily, she's...gone. She and Peter were killed when their car went off the road."

Preston felt Ivy's body go limp. He did his best to support her as she fell into him, but he felt a bit weak himself. He guided her to the front porch chair and held her in his arms, rocking back and forth. She started sobbing hysterically, wracked with pain over the loss of her only child. She stopped crying for a moment when she thought of little Laney, asleep on the sofa. *How can I possibly tell that sweet child that her parents are dead?*

Laney awoke from the commotion and wandered onto the front porch. Ivy attempted to collect herself, but Laney could see something was wrong.

"Grandma, are you crying?"

Ivy decided to be straightforward and truthful with her.

"Yes, Laney girl. I have something to tell you. Please come and sit by me."

Ivy told Laney that her mother and father had died and were not coming back. She waited for Laney to start asking questions. It helped to have Preston close by for moral support.

"Oh," was all Laney said.

"Is there anything you want to ask me, Laney girl?"

At four years old, Laney couldn't begin to understand the finality of death and the ramifications of losing her parents. All she wanted to know was where she would live and if she could bring her dolls with her. Ivy embraced her and reassured Laney that she would live with her and could bring all her things.

Laney's innocence and immaturity in dealing with grief granted Ivy a temporary reprieve. She knew there would be tears and heartache once the full gravity of the situation began to sink in. Somehow, they would survive this terrible tragedy together.

June 11, 1968

Dear Diary,

The loss of a child is almost too much to bear. I cannot believe I will never see my dear Lily again, hear her voice, or hold her in my arms. A piece of my heart and soul has died along with Lily, and this unescapable heartache surpasses how badly I felt when Hank was killed. The only thing that keeps me going is my responsibility to raise my granddaughter. She is all I live for now. At times, I wonder if God is punishing me for something I've done.

Due to the horrific nature of the way Lily and Peter died, no viewing was held, only a graveside service. After the priest gave his final blessing over Lily's casket, Ivy and Laney walked hand in hand to the car that waited to take them back to her house. Preston followed behind them.

They drove back to Ivy's house for the small gathering of friends and family who came to the funeral for Lily. No one came to mourn Peter's passing. Ivy could not bear the thought of having Peter buried next to Lily and Hank in the family plot. Instead, Peter's body was laid to rest in a gravesite near his father's. For the first time since Lily's death, Ivy allowed herself a small measure of relief —Peter would trouble them no longer.

In the days and weeks following the funeral, Ivy tried to keep Laney's routine unchanged. Each morning she dressed the little girl, fixed her breakfast, and walked her out to the yard to play as she always had.

Some nights Laney would wake up and call for her mother. Ivy would gather her into her arms and rock her until the tears subsided. Rarely did the child ask for Peter.

When Laney finally drifted back to sleep, Ivy often remained awake, sitting quietly beside the bed with her own grief pressing heavily on her heart.

Soon after their deaths, Ivy visited the law firm of Gallagher & Gallagher to make arrangements to legally adopt Laney. Ivy thought it best that Laney keep her last name, Armstrong, at least for now. Mr. Gallagher said she could have it changed at a later date, perhaps when Laney entered school if any issues arose from them having different last names.

Laney followed Ivy everywhere she went. She absorbed everything Ivy taught her, like making a bed, cooking meals, and tending to the garden. She gave Laney little tasks to complete and praised her accomplishments. Laney learned lessons on how to be self-sufficient and confident. Ivy felt as if she had been given a second chance at raising a child and took great care to do a good job.

One afternoon, while working in the garden with Laney, Ivy realized something had been missing that spring. Being preoccupied with the funeral and getting Laney settled in, Ivy neglected to notice that Herb Martin had not returned this year to work for her. Being a drifter without a permanent address, Ivy had no way to contact him. He never spoke much about himself, saying only that he hailed from Florida. She didn't even know if he had a family. She hoped nothing had happened to him.

Chapter Twenty-Four

West Ashley, SC – 1989

"I T SURE IS A pretty day outside," Billy Buchanan's nurse aide said. "How about letting me wheel you down to the gazebo so you can enjoy the sunshine?"

"No thanks. I'm fine right here."

The aide left the room shaking her head. Every day, she tried to get Billy to leave his room, but he sat in his wheelchair and stared out the window. It seemed something was weighing heavily on his mind.

When Billy met Laney at her wedding, he knew she would want to visit and ask questions he didn't want to answer. But maybe the time had come to let go of the lies and secrets he'd kept bottled up for decades. Billy welcomed the chance to come clean and clear his conscience. What would be so bad about that? It's not like he'd done anything wrong. It was just an unfortunate circumstance.

Not wanting to think about it anymore, he nodded off to sleep in his chair. His fitful nap echoed screams, shouts, and images that had frequented his dreams for so many years. He awoke in a cold sweat.

Billy tried to recount the events of that fateful night in his head. After all these years, he wondered if he contrived his own version of the story to make himself feel better about what had really happened. No one could verify the facts except him. Preston, the only other person who knew the truth, died several years ago. Billy never expected Peter Armstrong's daughter to start nosing around, asking questions about her father's death. If Ivy hadn't divulged in her letter that Laney's father might not be dead after all, none of this would be happening right now. Wasn't it enough that he had to live with the secret for so long while the rest of the town spoke of the tragic deaths of "that beautiful young couple," making him cringe every time he heard the words?

Laney, Chase, and his mom were escorted to Uncle Billy's room. It was bright and cheery with a large window overlooking a pond. His nurse had let him know about the visit when his family called, and he'd agreed to see them.

Billy knew the day of reckoning had arrived. He hoped the exchange would free his burdened soul. As the nurse led them into the room, she recommended they speak loudly and slowly since his hearing wasn't very good.

Chase greeted his uncle. "Hello, Uncle Billy," he said, reaching out to shake his uncle's hand.

"Chase, my boy. So good to see you again. How's married life treating you?"

"Just fine. You remember Laney."

"Hello, Uncle Billy. How are you?" asked Laney as she bent down to peck his cheek with a kiss.

"Much better now," quipped Billy.

"Hello, Marjorie, you're looking as beautiful as ever."

Marjorie gave him a hug and thanked him for the compliment.

"I have an idea why you're here, and I want you to know that I'll do my best to answer any questions you have. Everything happened a long time ago, but there are some things a man remembers his whole life." A sadness tinged his eyes as he stared vacantly out the window.

"I appreciate you helping me learn the truth about my father, and I'll understand if it's too painful to talk about. It's just that you're the only one who can help exonerate my grandmother."

"Ivy?" he asked in an astounded tone. "She had nothing to feel guilty about!"

Laney needed to know more. "Please, Uncle, tell us about that night." They all listened as Uncle Billy began to retell the whole sordid event.

"Petey drew the short straw from the minute he was born. His father worked little jobs here and there. His mother took off and left them, leaving Petey to spend most of his life on his own. A boy needs someone to show him the way, but he had no one. We all thought Lily Westfield was too good for Petey but hoped she would make an honest man of him. When the drinking got out of control, so did he.

"When Petey showed up to extort money from Ivy, Preston asked me to help. Preston and I went back a long way, and I owed him many favors over the years.

"Preston had arranged to meet Petey near the river to give him money to get rid of him for good, but he asked me to go in his stead. It was darker than usual that night, no trace of the moon or stars in the black sky.

"Petey seemed nervous and fidgety. He was surprised I was there and not Preston, but was so eager to get the money that he didn't put up a fuss. I offered him a swig of moonshine, and he gulped it down like a man who'd been in the desert too long. I told him that Preston didn't want to see his face in these parts anymore, and he should make plans to leave town as fast as he could. It didn't matter where he went, just as long as he got out of town immediately.

"Petey didn't like being threatened and, with the help of the bottle, became quite brazen and asked what Preston was going to do about it if he didn't leave.

"Preston had given me permission to do whatever I had to do to convince Petey to skedaddle. I hate to admit it, but I had sort of a soft spot for that fella because he was dealt a bum hand. I tried to reason with him, but he wanted no part of it.

"Next thing I knew, he pulled a gun out of his pocket and started waving it in the air. I told him to put it away, and no one would get hurt. One thing led to another, and Petey lunged at me with the gun pointed right at my head. I ducked out of the way and swung back around, caught his right arm, and twisted it behind his back. But he was too quick for me.

"He took the gun in his left hand, reached back, and dug it into my side. I managed to kick his legs out from underneath him, hoping both he and the gun would fall to the ground. Well, it didn't go as planned. He fell alright, but his finger was on the trigger, and the gun went off, right into his chest. Thick red blood dripped from his body. He managed to get up, staggered a few feet, and then fell over, right into the river. The current was strong from the rain the night before, and I watched his lifeless body get carried away. I suspect the water carried him all the way out to the ocean because his body was never found."

Sweat ran down the side of Uncle Billy's face during his recounting of that fateful night. Laney got him a glass of water and handed him his handkerchief that had fallen silently to the floor while he was talking. It took a lot out of him to recall the terrible memory.

A wide range of emotions flooded her mind: sorrow, anger, grief, horror. She imagined her father's lifeless body floating down the river. She stood up and felt a little lightheaded. Chase quickly ran to her side and ushered her to a nearby chair. Marjorie brought Laney a glass of water and sat on her other side, holding her hand.

"We're here for you, my dear."

"Maybe we should stop for today," said Chase.

"No, I'm okay. But I do have a few questions. Why didn't anyone report my father's death?"

"Petey had already been pronounced dead from the car accident and was presumably buried in his father's plot. Only Ivy and Preston knew that he had returned. Preston didn't want me to be implicated in Petey's death, so we never said a word about him coming back to extort money from Ivy."

"But if it wasn't my father in the car, who was it?"

"I wondered the same thing. The corpse was so badly charred that all the coroner had to go on was the wallet he found next to the car that belonged to Petey. Although I heard something odd a few weeks later. Chuck—that's the coroner—and I were having a few beers, and he mentioned to me that the body only had three fingers on one hand. As far as I can remember, Petey didn't have any missing fingers."

"That was Herb Martin...," Laney said as a distant memory came to the surface, "one of the seasonal hands my grandmother employed every year."

"What makes you think it was him?"

"I was the one who caused Herb to lose two fingers in a barn accident."

"What happened?" asked Uncle Billy curiously.

"I was climbing down from the loft when my foot got caught in the ladder rung. Herb was working at his tool bench and saw me start to fall. He ran over and caught me before I hit the ground, and sat me in a chair, but didn't see the ladder falling behind him. It came crashing down, knocking several tools off their hooks, including a machete, which sliced through Herb's left hand."

"That must have been terrifying for a little girl."

"It was. I felt horrible that I caused him to lose his fingers. But being the sweet man he was, he never blamed me."

"Well, I'll be darned. You came to me for answers, but instead, you solved a mystery that has haunted me for years."

It sickened Laney that Herb had been killed in a senseless accident, and her father had used an innocent man to cover up his role in the death of Laney's mother.

It was all too much to bear, and Laney broke into tears. She cried for her grandmother, her mother, and, strangely enough, even her father. She cried for herself and for the years of growing up without her parents.

Chase drew her into his arms and let the waves of tears flow. Laney needed to grieve all the losses in her life and process this new information that finally provided the answers she'd been searching for. Chase would help her work through her grief in hopes that they could move on with their lives together. Laney gained her composure, and suddenly, her eyes opened wide and she smiled.

"Lane, are you okay?" Chase asked, confused by the sudden change in her demeanor.

"Yes. I just realized something. In the letter from my grandmother, she expressed the guilt she carried with her throughout her life, thinking she may have played a part in causing harm to my father. But now we know, she didn't. His death was accidental and self-inflicted. She didn't have anything to do with it. I just wish she were alive to know all this."

Chapter Twenty-Five

Charleston, SC – 1989

LANEY REPLAYED THE CONVERSATION with Uncle Billy in her head all night long. She wanted to somehow feel closer to her mother and Ivy. The next morning, she awoke at five with Chase snoring lightly beside her. Not wanting to disturb him, she quietly slipped out of bed, got dressed, and went downstairs. Feeling a little queasy, she decided to skip breakfast. Laney left a note on the kitchen table: "Chase, I took a drive to the beach, be back soon. Love, Laney."

Ambling along the sandy beach, Laney watched the orange sun rise majestically out of the water. She pictured walking hand in hand with Ivy as they often did together. Laney remembered bringing seashells to Ivy—pretty little treasures found after the tide retreated. Ivy would place them in her pocket for safekeeping, treating the shells as if they were precious gemstones.

Laney left the beach and went to the cemetery where Ivy and her mother had been buried. She cleaned up a few stray weeds that were overgrowing around the headstone. Sitting on the ground in front of the marker, she traced the names of her mother and grandmother engraved in the cold gray marble. Tears welled in her eyes, and Laney spoke to them as if they were right there in front of her.

"I miss you, Mama. Our time together was cut short, but your memory lingers in my heart. Grandma, you were my entire world, always there when I needed you. I miss you dearly and think of you every day. I understand and forgive you for keeping my father a secret from me, and doing what was needed to protect me.

"It was the right thing to do. I pray you can absolve yourself of any guilt or wrongdoing because you acted purely out of love and concern for me. I'm eternally grateful for all you have given me, and I love you so much."

Laney felt a warm breeze enveloping her body. The overwhelming sensation was as comforting as being wrapped in a thick, fluffy blanket on a cold winter's day. Laney rose from the grass and felt a little dizzy. Grabbing the headstone for support, she righted herself and walked back to the car.

She thought perhaps she needed a little breakfast to boost her energy.

Chase sat on the front porch holding a cup of coffee in his hand. He looked so relaxed in a worn-out sweatshirt and faded blue jeans, his hair tousled from last night's slumber. Rascal barely lifted his head to greet her as she walked up the steps.

"Hi there. I was beginning to wonder when you'd be coming home. You okay, Lane?"

Laney bent down to give Chase a kiss on the forehead and sat beside him on the chair next to his. "Yes. I went to visit Mama and Grandma in the cemetery."

"Did it help?"

"Actually, it did. There were some things I needed to say to them."

"You've been through a lot, Lane. I'm here to listen if you want to talk about it."

"I told them both how much I loved them and felt a sense of closure, but I don't have any closure when it comes to my father."

"I'm not sure what we can do about that. Uncle Billy said his body was never recovered."

"That's the part I'm having a difficult time reconciling in my head. Do you think it showed up somewhere but wasn't identified?"

"I suppose that's a possibility."

"What happens when a body is found, and no one claims it?"

"I'm not entirely sure, but I've seen notices in the newspaper from the coroner's office in search of next of kin for unclaimed bodies."

"We would need to look through records from the year my father returned to extort money from my grandmother. Maybe we can try searching at the Charleston Public library. They have microfilm archives of old newspapers."

"Good idea. I'll get dressed, and we can go now."

They drove to the Charleston County Main Library on Calhoun Street. The librarian led them to the room that housed the microfilm records for newspaper articles. She gave them a quick lesson on how to operate the machine and wished them luck in finding what they were looking for. They loaded the first reel of film and began their search.

Laney scanned through page after page for anything that might be a clue. After an hour, Chase turned to Laney and said, "This might be like trying to find a needle in a haystack."

"I know. This process is very tedious. I don't mind staying here alone if there's something else you'd rather do."

"No, it's okay. Maybe we can take turns so you don't get cross-eyed trying to read the small print."

"That's a deal."

They continued for a few hours when Chase said, "I could use a burger. How 'bout you, Lane?"

"Sure. I'm starving and need to stretch my legs."

After lunch, they walked around the town in Charleston for a short while before returning to the library. The search seemed futile until an article caught Laney's eye.

"Chase, I think I might have found something."

"What is it?"

"There's a front-page article here about a father and son who were fishing near Sullivan's Island, right across the bay."

Chase peered over her shoulder to get a better look at the screen. "That doesn't sound very interesting."

"Keep reading. While fishing, they discovered a body stuck on the rocks in the shallow water. The police were called in, and the body was taken to the morgue. There was a gunshot wound to the chest."

"Now *that* is interesting."

According to the article, "South Carolina law requires county coroners to arrange for the burial of unidentified or unclaimed bodies in the county in which the remains were found. Burial will take place, and additional information, such as photos, identifying marks, and DNA, may be logged and stored by the municipality."

"The article says that no one claimed the body, so it was buried in the county cemetery by the coroner."

"We need to take this article to the sheriff's office to check and see if any information was recorded."

"I guess that's our next stop." They printed a copy of the article and gathered their things to leave.

The sheriff directed Laney and Chase to the detective in charge of cold cases.

"Hello. I'm Detective Tom Meyers. I hear you may have information about an unclaimed body."

"That's correct, sir," replied Laney. "I believe the man in question may have been my father." She went on to explain the circumstances surrounding Peter's death and the initial car accident to the detective.

"I appreciate you coming forward with this information, Mrs. Buchanan. I know this must be very difficult for you."

"Yes, but I'm hoping to put this whole ordeal to rest."

"Agreed. It's always best to resolve cases such as these for the sake of all the families involved. I must warn you, though, that some of the evidence can be difficult to view. For example, the photographs taken of the corpse are quite disturbing, given the fact that the body was in the water for a few days."

"I understand. I'm prepared to do whatever I have to do."

Chase put an arm around Laney for support as the detective opened the file.

"The victim was male, five feet ten inches tall, with brown hair and brown eyes, estimated between thirty and thirty-five years of age, with a gunshot wound to the chest. Other distinguishing features include a tattoo on the left upper forearm, *Lily*."

"These characteristics would match those of my father. I was too young to remember him having a tattoo, but Lily was my mother's name."

"Let's view the picture to help positively identify him."

"Okay. I have a picture of him with me if that would help."

"Yes, ma'am. That would definitely help with identification." The detective removed the photograph from the old case file, and Laney gasped. The face and body was bloated and somewhat distorted. She took out the faded picture of Peter from her purse and gave it to the detective for comparison. Although both weren't completely clear, there were enough resembling features to identify the body as Peter's.

"I believe we have a match."

"What happens now?" Chase asked the detective.

"Our department will issue a certified death certificate confirming the body buried in Magnolia Cemetery is indeed Peter Armstrong, and the headstone will be marked appropriately. That is, of course, unless you wish to move the body to a family plot."

Laney thought about it for a moment. Her mother and grandmother wouldn't have wanted Peter to be buried near them. "I don't wish to do that, sir," she said quietly.

"As you wish, ma'am. I'm sorry for your loss. Is there anything else I can do for you at this time?"

"Just one thing, Detective Meyers. Would you be able to search through missing persons records for Herbert Martin? The only information I have is that he was a drifter, possibly from Florida."

"Yes, I can do that for you. Our office uses the FBI's National Crime Information Center and the Social Security Death Index to cross-reference missing-person reports from all fifty states. It would include information back to 1968, the year you believe he died."

The search of the FBI records showed no missing-person report was filed for Herbert Martin, and the Social Security Death Index reported that no checks were issued or cashed in his name.

Laney barely spoke a word on the drive home. Chase gave her time to come to terms with all that had happened. It wasn't until later that evening that Laney was able to talk about it.

"Can I make you a cup of tea, Lane?"

"I would like that, Chase. Thank you for being so understanding. I know all of this hasn't been easy for you either."

"My only concern is you and helping you through it."

"I'm okay, honestly. In an odd sort of way, it's a relief to finally be able to lay my father to rest without having any nagging questions about what happened to him. I know, beyond a shadow of a doubt, that he is never coming back."

"I'm glad to hear you can be at peace with that knowledge."

"I am, Chase. There's just one more thing I need to do, but it can wait until tomorrow."

The next day, Chase drove Laney to the cemetery in town. She brought the documentation proving that Peter Armstrong was buried in Magnolia Cemetery and not in the plot with his name on the marker. She arranged to replace the headstone on the grave thought to be Peter's with a new one. It would have the simple inscription, "Herbert Martin. Rest in peace."

"Your grandmother would be so proud of you, Laney," Chase told her as they stood in front of Herb's grave.

"She taught me to do the right thing, no matter how hard it may be. I wanted to make things right for Herb. He was a sweet and kind man who helped her during the war. It's the least I could do for him."

"You are like Ivy in more ways than you realize. Family, honor, respect, and integrity are all a part of who you are and the reason why I love you so much."

"The same goes for you, Chase. Your parents may have set the examples, but you emulate those moral qualities in everything you do. I couldn't have done this without you by my side."

"And that is where you will always find me."

Chapter Twenty-Six

Charleston, SC – 1989

W HILE DOING A LITTLE light housecleaning, Laney accidentally knocked Ivy's diary off the dresser. As she reached down to pick the book up from the floor, she noticed it had opened to a page that Ivy had earmarked for some reason. She read the entry:

December 18, 1940

Dear Diary,
I'm in a family way.

Laney smiled at the naivety of her grandmother at such an early age. In those days, saying the word "pregnant" was not considered proper. *Things have certainly changed a lot since that time.*

She continued dusting and vacuuming but became woozy and needed to sit down. Chase found her sitting on the edge of the bed, looking pale and fatigued.

"Lane, what is it? Are you feeling sick?"

"I'm okay, it's just a little warm and stuffy in this room."

"Has this happened before?"

"A few times. Mostly after I first get up in the morning."

Suddenly, Laney realized what might be the cause. The upset stomach yesterday morning and dizziness this afternoon, it all began to add up.

She looked into Chase's eyes and told him, "I think I might be pregnant."

"Honest? You mean it, Lane?"

"Well, it's a little too soon to tell, and I can't be one hundred percent sure, but it's a very strong possibility."

Chase threw his arms around her and hugged her so tightly she nearly lost her breath. "I love you so much, Laney. This is the best news ever."

"I love you too. More than anything."

"Ivy would be so happy to know that you're expecting a baby. It would have meant the world to her that her great-granddaughter would be born in her house."

Laney thought about the earmarked passage in Ivy's diary. "Somehow, I have a feeling she knows, Chase," said Laney, a sparkle in her eye.

Dr. Porter confirmed what Laney suspected and handed her a printed appointment card for her next visit. Chase and Laney couldn't wait to tell the Buchanans that they were going to be grandparents and invited Marjorie and Joe to brunch the next morning.

Laney set a beautiful table outside on the back porch with a white linen tablecloth and a bouquet of fresh flowers in the center. She chose her grandmother's delicate bone china and cloth napkins for the place settings to honor Ivy. She would have appreciated the extra care and special touches Laney put forth on this momentous occasion.

Quiche Lorraine was her specialty, and Laney paired it with a cinnamon-spiced raisin walnut cake for dessert. As she put the finishing touches on the table, Chase snuck up behind her and put his arms around her. Laney let her head fall back and melt into Chase's shoulder, and she wrapped her arms around his.

"I love you, Lane."

Laney closed her eyes and said a silent prayer of thanks for this wonderful man whom she loved so much. "And I you, Chase."

He slid his hands to Laney's midsection. "And baby makes three."

Laney smiled at the thought of the two of them becoming a little family soon. The warmth and soft glow of the morning sun surrounded them, and they took a moment to enjoy the peacefulness.

"Hello? Anybody home?" Marjorie called out as she breezed through the front door.

"We're out here, Mom."

Joe and Marjorie were right on time and brought some fresh-baked pastries.

"Where shall I put these, dear?"

"I thought we'd eat outside since it's such a beautiful morning."

"My, my, what an elegant table," exclaimed Marjorie. "What's the special occasion?"

She looked directly at Laney and noticed the corners of her mouth curl into a smile and the twinkle in her eye. Joe took a seat at the table, unfazed by the pretty presentation.

"I'm hungry this morning. What smells so good?"

"Never mind that, Joe, I think Laney and Chase have something to tell us."

Knowing Marjorie, Laney wasn't surprised by her motherly intuition.

"Is it what I think it is, Laney?"

Unable to contain her excitement, she shouted, "Yes, I'm pregnant!"

Marjorie let out an ecstatic cry and embraced both Laney and Chase at the same time. Tears of joy streamed down her face. Joe got up from the table and shook his son's hand.

"Congratulations, my boy. That's wonderful news!" he said. Joe gave Laney a bear hug and planted a kiss on her cheek. "Well, little lady, you're gonna be a mama," he said, fighting back a few tears himself.

All through breakfast, they talked about the arrival of the baby. He or she would be born sometime in late September. Chase and Joe would convert the spare bedroom back into a nursery like Hank and Ivy had done for Lily. Joe promised to dig out Chase's rocking horse and start refinishing it.

Laney chuckled at their unbridled enthusiasm over their first grandchild. She knew that this baby, and his or her future siblings, would grow up safe and secure in a happy home, surrounded by a loving family. The sound of children's laughter would breathe new life into the house on Cypress Lane, and Ivy's legacy would continue. There would be birthday and holiday parties, picnics by the pond, fireworks on the Fourth of July, and the school bus would add a new stop at the end of the driveway.

The past few days were a whirlwind of emotions for Laney. She felt overwhelming joy at the news of the baby, coupled with anxiety and fear about becoming a mother. *How will I know what to do? Will the baby be healthy? Will I be a good mom?*

Laney wished Ivy and Lily could be there when she needed help in her role as a new mother. Of course, Marjorie would step in and support her, but she longed for the comfort and care of her own mother and grandmother. Needing to find a little reassurance, Laney picked up Ivy's diary and searched for any entries that might offer insight into how she and Lily felt about motherhood. She found exactly what she was looking for.

February 19, 1964

Dear Diary,

Watching Lily with her new baby is reminiscent of how I felt those first few days after becoming a new mother. My own mother seldom demonstrated her love for me, and, as any child would, I craved affection. I spent countless nights worrying about my ability to be a good mother. I was pleasantly surprised and relieved when my motherly intuition shone through. I see the same qualities in Lily. She is so at ease with Laney, and despite all the trepidation she felt during her pregnancy, she seems to have taken well to motherhood. When Lily gazes into her baby's eyes, it's as if I'm watching myself as a new mother.

Laney immediately felt reassured and comforted. If her grandmother and her mother could raise a child in the face of all the adversity and strife in their lives, then she could too, especially with Chase by her side.

EPILOGUE

Charleston, SC – 2026

LANEY SAT ON THE front porch swing, watching the children playing in the front yard. She loved these late summer evenings when the sun began to set a little earlier each day. Fall, her favorite time of year, was right around the corner, and the holidays wouldn't be too far behind.

Laney loved the changing colors of the leaves and the cooler weather. She enjoyed decorating the house, baking seasonal favorites for the children, and shopping for special gifts for each of them for Christmas. Just the thought of all the preparations and decorations sent her heart racing with excitement and anticipation.

She and Chase were fulfilling the dream that her mother and grandmother Ivy always wanted but never had: a house full of children's laughter, special moments and memories, and an abundance of joy and love. Of course, there were some rough patches, a few illnesses, bumps and bruises, but all in all, they shared a wonderful life together.

As Laney took a sip of her iced tea, one of the children ran up the stairs and jumped up on her lap. Her clothes were damp from taking a dip in the pond after playing on the swing. Laney didn't care in the least and welcomed the sweet child into her arms. She was only seven years old, but Laney could already see that she was a spitfire and had the same grit and determination that all the Westfield women before her had possessed.

"Tell me the story again, please!" the little girl begged.

Laney must have told her the story at least one hundred times, but never tired of retelling it.

"Okay, Ivy dear," she told her granddaughter, "I will tell you all about your great-great-grandmother Ivy."

Laney always started the story the same way. "This big, beautiful house on Cypress Lane has seen the love and growth of five generations of Westfields, and you, little Ivy, were named after its matriarch."

She continued recounting the lives and times of Ivy, Lily, and herself, answering the dozens of questions that little Ivy asked about each of them.

"Tell me about my mama and her brothers and sisters," begged Ivy.

"Your mother, Lyla, was the first child your grandpa and I welcomed into our family, followed by Susannah, and William, or little Billy as we call him. So that means you have an aunt, an uncle, and several cousins. Your mama loved being the big sister to her siblings and still does."

Just then, Chase walked up the sidewalk and sat beside them.

"Grandma is telling me the house story!"

"Again? You must know it by heart."

"Yeah, but I like hearing her tell it."

Chase leaned back in his rocking chair and listened to the sweet sound of his wife's voice while remembering the night he came to her rescue on the side of the road and how both of their lives had changed forever. It seemed like a lifetime ago at times...and only yesterday at others.

Laney peered into Chase's eyes, reading his thoughts. As Ivy drifted off to sleep, Laney and Chase sat together peacefully, watching the setting sun, contemplating how their story would continue with the next generation.

ABOUT THE AUTHOR

Janine Lange is an award-winning, international author who blends her love of history with a gift for storytelling. She writes engaging, heartfelt historical fiction that brings the past to life through richly drawn characters and emotionally resonant journeys. Her novels explore the strength of family bonds, the power of resilience, and the enduring nature of love, often weaving together themes of legacy, hope, and second chances.

When she isn't writing, Janine enjoys cooking, gardening, reading, crocheting, traveling, and spending time with family—simple pleasures that often inspire the warmth and authenticity found in her stories. She is passionate about connecting with readers and sharing stories that linger in the heart long after the final page. Follow Janine and explore her work at: **janinelange.com**.